The Book at the Bar

Kirahvi Bello

To the people that enjoy reading smut in public without judgement

The Book at the Bar

Contents

The Book at the Bar

Contents

Playlist

Stuck by Durand Bernarr ft. Ari Lennox
Hottie by Flo Milli ft. Babyface Ray
Downtown by SVW
Facetime by Ari Lennox
Brown Sugar by D'Angelo
Beep Me 911 by Missy Elliott
Sometimes Dancin' by Brownstone
Me and You by Tony! Toni! Tone!
Mary's Joint by Mary J Blige
Brown Skin by India Arie
My Place by Tweet
Calling on You by Jon B.
(Lay Your Head on My) Pillow by Tony! Toni! Tone!
Felt This Way by Indigo Mak
An Idea by IAMNOBODI ft. Emmavie, Zacar & Josh J
Find my Way to Love by Jaspects ft. Chantae Cann
Mo' Better Blues by Bransford Marsalis Quartet & Terrence Blanchard
Misty by Samara Joy
Let Me Prove My Love to You by the Main Ingredient
Confession by Budgie
Can I Get Your Name by Angela Munoz & Adrian Younge
Creole by Charlie Hunter Quartet
The Panties by Mos Def
Come Back to Me by Janet Jackson
Certainly by Erykah Badu
If I Was Your Man by Joe
The Peacocks by Bill Evans Trio
Sunset and the Mocking Bird (The Queen's Suite) by Duke Ellington & His Orchestra
Summer's Over Interlude by Drake
Insane by Summer Walker
Summer Renaissance by Beyonce
I'm that Girl by Beyonce

Before you read, this is a novel with explicitly detailed sex scenes.

Chapter One

Calvin

Damn, why did they fold the corner of the pages? That is so disrespectful. These books have gone through so much already." He rubbed his thumb in-between his eyebrows, the stress of a librarian. He gathered all of the books from the drop off box and began individually observing and sorting them. He carefully placed them on his cart to be scanned then returned back on the shelves.

He's owned this library for over a year, and has healed his inner child while being there. Everything had to be perfect with him in charge, especially with being one of the few black men in the field. He's finally fully staffed which has helped plan donation drives, reading circles and create book displays for a variety of ages and genres. He even built the 'Books for the Beach' display with real sand, since it was the summer. Unfortunately, the only 'real' body of water close by was haunted. *Do not go to Lake Lanier.* There were still other things that need to be handled, like the Steven King novel on his desk and his nonexistent social life. But besides that, his dream job had become a well-oiled machine, predictable and reliable.

After Calvin vacuumed the elevator tracks and wiped down the tables and chairs, one of his best friends and co-owner, Greg, suggested he check out a bar close by. Calvin was never really a bar kind of guy. They were loud, dirty and people would be in your personal space. Why would he pretend to interact with 'humans' when the perfect people were in his books? Nobody asked him about his family or any deeply personal questions. He'd never gone to one and had a 'special' moment anyway. His phone buzzed in his pocket.

Greg: You're going to that bar tonight whether you like it or not.

Calvin: ….

Greg: You need to spend time outside, time with REAL people

Calvin: Yea I know. Can't wait to stand in a crowded room with other sweaty people to drink drinks I can make at home

Greg: Try it for at least an hour bro please. I'm worried about you. Promise?

Calvin: I promise

He sighed as he stuffed his phone back in his pocket. He appreciated Greg's friendship. He's known him since high school and trusted his opinion. Greg was one of the few people that reminded him that the outside world existed. Who knows what might happen at the bar? At least he'll drain a few glasses of whiskey and keep to himself. It's easy to blend into a crowd. Calvin wasn't really the "join another man friend group" type. The last time Calvin went bar hopping with Greg, it didn't end well. Greg had to carry him to his car, which strangely put butterflies in the stomach, apart from the alcohol.

Calvin had to admit, he loved being swept off his feet by Greg. The way he smelled, how easily he went into the air and how the rare Atlanta sun hit his face. Maybe if he bit him then, he could excuse it as him 'being drunk.' They have had some interesting moments together. Calvin mentioned his bisexuality to Greg when they were smoking outside of a party in college. They just stared at each other, not saying another word. Nothing was said after that, so Calvin acted like he never said anything. He chose the friendship over pushing it. If Greg was homophobic, he wouldn't still be his friend, right?

Before he left the library, Calvin paid the bills, dusted his office and read a few chapters. After he ordered another rug for reading time, since a kid threw up and the stain wouldn't lift, he slowly began packing his satchel and locked his office. If anyone but Greg told him about the bar, it would be an immediate no.

Greg: Stop stalling nigga

Calvin rolled his eyes as he turned off the lights and locked the front door. When he searched his GPS, the bar was just up the street.

One hour that's it.

He already decided that he wasn't going to talk to anyone. It would have to take divine intervention.

Chapter Two

Gemini

Hello! Thank you for calling Helping Human Helpers, your HR expert here. How many I help you?" She said rolling her eyes. *I need my Friday bar escape now more than ever.* She thought to herself while listening to the person yell in her ear about their missing paycheck. Being on the phone all day was taking a toll on her mind. She imagined the curse words flying over her head and smacking her in the face.

All calls are recorded anyway.

After Gemini sent the customer an email with the Missing Pay form including thorough instructions and a request for a survey, the caller hung up thanking her.

While typing her call notes, a high pitched voice yelped behind her. "Hey Gemini!" Her eager boss said with a smile standing in her cube. "How are ya?"

Gemini forced a smile after being cursed out for 10 minutes. "I'm fine Jane. You?"

Jane smiled so wide that her pale skin wrinkled by her eyes.

"Oh at least it's Friday! I'm headed out soon. I just assigned 7 cases to you. They are all questions about HHH polices and you are the in house expert! Can you take care of those for me?"

Gemini exhaled, the fake smile still painted on her face. *Go to your happy place, you need this job.* "Sure Jane, I'll take care of it. Have a good weekend." She said dryly. "But I'll have to be off the phone lines to focus."

Jane nodded, "Of course! Anything to get it done. Thank you hun! You have a good weekend too." Then Jane's phone rang and she was on the move again. Her black pin skirt and stilettos tiptoed towards the door. Gemini had one hour to do three hours of work. Luckily, she does have most of the Helping Human Helpers policies memorized so it didn't take long to answer the questions and close the cases. It was still a pain having to search each policy though. Policies can change in a matter of hours from one big wig meeting. If the paperwork doesn't back up what you say, then you have to pay.

As soon as the clock stuck 5, she logged out, closed her laptop and threw it in her work bag. Then locked her headset in her drawer. She waved bye to her coworkers and swiftly went down the elevators. She looked at herself in the elevator reflection. Her yellow button down had a few wrinkles and her dark Levi jeans hugged her in the right places. Then she yanked out her hair tie, her auburn braids fell and waved down her body past her waist. She took a deep breath as the doors opened, *ladies and gentleman, the weekend.*

She pulled into the bar parking lot, screaming *Hottie by Flo Milli* at the top of her lungs. The perfect time to go was right after work because after 8 o'clock, the 'fun' people filled up the place with noise. But, if you go right when the bar opens, it's dead empty. She sat down in her usual seat. Her burning braids rested at her waist as she sat on the bar stool. Gemini always sat at the corner so that she could see all doors. She hated when people snuck up behind her.

She took a deep breath, taking in the smell of cigarettes from the woman outside. Finally, no more ringing, random questions, last minute requests or reviewing forms. She got her Bachelor's degree in Business Management. But after taking a course in Human Resources, she knew that was the career path for her. It was the perfect blend of helping people in an ever changing industry. She wanted to know everything she could to be an HR director one day. So when Helping Human Helpers, the premier multibillion dollar Human Resource company came to her campus for a career fair; she interviewed with them and had a guaranteed job waiting for her after graduation. Now Gemini has been with the company 5 years and she was ready to be promoted.

The bartender was cleaning a glass as he walked over to her. She began pulling out her wallet and book out of her Tan crossbody bag. Yes she read at the bar, everyone has to have an escape. Hers was in a book. People are also less likely to bother you when there's a book in your hand. At least that's what her aunt advised her to stop fighting in elementary school. "Strawberry Daquiri Gem?" the bartender asked.

"You know it Al." The Georgia humidity was so thick, she could feel the hot wet air resting on her skin. Summer was in full speed in Atlanta, and she didn't like it. The frozen Strawberry

Daquiri would not be baby sat for long. She texted her closest friend, Serena.

Gemini: Made it to the bar sis. Love you!

Serena Main One: Okay love you and be safe! Keep your drink close

Serena was the first friend she made when she moved to Valdosta as a kid. They had countless sleepovers and navigated everything together from learning how to shave to Twilight marathons. They even went to the same college because they couldn't imagine being apart. But when Gemini decided to move to Atlanta for her now ex, Serena moved to New York for graduate school. They always did text checks when they went out in public in case one of them went missing. At least it gave somewhere to start.

Gemini opened her book just as Al set her drink down on the napkin in front of her. She nodded to him and began reading her romance novel. With her drink in one hand and a book in the other, she absorbed herself into her paradise. It was the closest she could ever get to the kind of relationship she dreamt of. Boy met girl, fuck multiple times, fall in love and live happily ever after.

Sadly, book characters got more play than she did. She hadn't had sex in three years, since her cheating ungrateful ex-boyfriend. Since then, she swore off men, not that anyone else was in line to attack her anyway. She has been doing a good enough job making herself cum. As some say, 'batteries are a girls best friend'.

The single life had become simple and easier. She enjoyed coming home to her cat, Constance, and cooking dinner for one. The only messes that existed, were of her own doing. There were no random pair of socks peeking out from under the dresser or shoes thrown across the living room. Everything had a place. Gemini preferred a reality where she was in control, not listen to someone tell her what to do and when to do it. So living alone it was.

As people walked in, she enjoyed occasionally looking up and observing them. The couples that came together, the single people that sat at the outdoor tables and stared at their phones. She liked when people were around her but didn't talk to her. That's why she read in public spaces. It allowed her to people watch with no interference.

The book, her wall to hide behind.

Two hours passed before she noticed. Her cup was empty and she had only 50 pages left in the novel. It was dark outside but she sat under a blue neon light that lit her pages just enough. She looked around the room again and noticed a pair of eyes looking back at her. She squinted. Maybe he wasn't looking at her, but past her. Nobody ever paid her any attention.

She looked down, then back up to him. He was still looking at her. His dark chocolate skin gleamed under the colorful lights above the bar. He grinned at her, his pearly whites flashing at her from across the room. She half grinned, looking back down, tucking her braids behind her ears. Maybe if she ignored him, he would leave her alone. She didn't come to bars to find men; she came to read her book. But he was fine though and he's wearing sexy ass glasses. Even though he smiled from a distance, she wanted to know what his lips tasted like. *That's the horniness talking, we're gonna ignore that.*

She wouldn't dare approach him. She was the weird black woman sitting at the corner of the bar reading smut. *Please don't walk over here. Please don't walk over here.* She couldn't bring herself to look up yet and see if he was still there. She gripped her book and slowly closed it. She looked up and he was gone. She began searching the room with her eyes. Where did he go?

"Hi," the warm deep voice said next to her.

Gemini jumped startled, thankful the music was just loud enough to cover her yelp. "Um hi, hello," she yelled with awkward chuckle. He was even more devastating up close. He looked 90s fine. He was *'I'm the blues in your left thigh, trying to become the funk in your right,'* fine. She could see his shoulder and chest muscles, a gold Cuban link chain gleamed on top of a crisp black t-shirt, with no wrinkles. It hugged his chest just enough for Gemini to stare. His thick black rimmed glasses made her want to yank them off his face. She hoped he would turn around so that she could at least see if he had an ass. But his face was good enough for now.

Then he did that honeypot melting smile again, right in her face. His lips looked just as good as she hoped. "I'm sorry I've been wanting to introduce myself all night but didn't want to disturb your reading. My name is Calvin, Cal for short. What's yours?" The right side of his lips lifted, his hand extended towards her.

She froze. This was a stranger, no matter how sittable his face looked. Should she tell him her real name? Should she just get up from the bar? A man hasn't shown interest in her in years. She should leave, just get in her car and leave. *Wait.* She hasn't paid her tab yet. The dark brown eyes standing next to her looked at her, waiting for an answer as his hand hung in the air. The walls hummed with the music around them.

She stretched her arm and shook his warm moisturized hand, a small surge of electricity shot through her. He was electric. Not just in his eyes, but in his touch too. "Uhhh my name is Gemini and sorry I was just leaving." She quickly let his hand go and waved over the bartender as she put her book back in her bag. He nodded to her.

"Leaving?" His eyes changed to more of a look of concern. A face that kissable shouldn't frown. "Am I disturbing you? I really didn't mean to. I've read that book and I'm a big fan of the author. I wanted to know how you liked it so far. Genuinely."

Huh. She looked at him up and down and arched her eyebrow. She pulled the book back out and showed him the cover of the book. "You read romance? But you're a man, not to be sexist or anything."

He chuckled as he looked away and back to her. "Yea I do actually, I love a variety of book genres, but romance is one of my favorites, next to fantasy or horror. I'm not pushing or anything. I just wanted to know if you wanted to talk about the book honestly. I'm a librarian so I could talk about books all day."

She blinked at him again. A librarian. A black, male, glasses wearing, sexy ass librarian? Walked into this bar and approached her. Was this a book boyfriend turned to life? The bartender walked over. "Everything okay Gemini? Want to close out your tab?" He glanced over at Calvin and looked at her again in the eye. "Do you need an Angel shot?"

She looked over at Calvin, the random handsome chocolate black man standing by her stool, and back to Al. What did she have to lose getting to know him? He didn't give off creep energy, more of a sexy LeVar Burton. "No I'll take another strawberry daiquiri outside." She smiled as she eyed Calvin up and down. Al nodded and turned away to start her drink.

Then she looked at Calvin in his eyes, he looked back at her like she was a shinning piece of gold. It made her legs twitch, they needed to go somewhere to continue their conversation. She just became aware of the loud music. "It's kind of loud in here. Are you good with sitting outside with me?"

He smiled "Ye- yea I'm cool with that." Her back was starting to sweat and it wasn't just the humidity.

She put her finger up. "If you try to kill me or drug my drink, I will kill you. Then, go to the funeral and act a fool again. Do we have an understanding?" She tapped the side of her bag. Even though all she had was a taser, she could still do some damage.

Calvin nodded putting his hands up "I don't want any trouble, lead the way." She looked him in the eye as she slid off the seat. It wasn't until she got off the bar stool that she realized they stood close to the same height. She didn't mind. She was 5'7", he seemed close to 5'9".

She headed outside, he wasn't far behind her. He held open the door for her to the back bar patio overlooking the parking lot and busy intersection. She chose the lounge couches with orange covers. She was scooting past the table about to sit down. "Wait before you sit down." She looked at him confused, he grabbed napkins from the table and wiped the seat, the bottom and the cushion. She sat down with an inquisitive look as he smiled back at her. He made sure her seat was clean? *How considerate?*

"So, you just wiped down my seat, do you have OCD or something?"

He laughed, the rolling sound made her grin. "No, I just didn't want your clothes to get dirty or anything. That is a beautiful top and I didn't want anything to get ruined. You are too beautiful to sit in dirt."

She scoffed and blushed. "I wore this to work, have to take advantage of jean day. But thanks anyway." He sat down on the couch about three cushions away from her. *Good. He better keep his distance.* She didn't know if she should punch him for mentioning books, the one thing she enjoyed talking about or kiss him. She hoped her drink was coming soon so she could hold something in her hands to keep her busy.

There was an awkward silence as they glanced at each other and the parking lot. She was about to open her book again. He kept looking at her. Why did he keep looking at her like that? Like she was a gift. "I'm sorry if I'm coming off awkward. I didn't think you would stay and talk to me."

She arched her eyebrows. Is that an insecurity being vocalized? "Why what makes you say that?"

He took a deep breath and rubbed his hands together. "I don't know," he opened his hands and closed them. He looked like he wished he didn't say anything.

Gemini looked at him confused. "You don't know? I don't get what you're saying. You look fine to me. I also stayed because you mentioned the one thing I enjoy talking about. So, maybe today is your lucky day." She said with a shrug.

He looked down at his hands and back in her eyes, it made her take a deep breath. What was going through his mind? "Okay, forget I said anything. How far along are you in the book?" He smiled at her in a way that made Gemini think he would actually care about her, which they both knew was a lie. How did he keep looking at her like this? Like he was studying her.

"I have 50 pages left. It's at a really juicy part too. I love how she writes. It feels like it's written just for me honestly. I love books with two lead black characters. It's easier to insert myself into the story you know? I feel like I'm hanging out with them."

He nodded, "Yea I do get that. I love watching how the story develops, while getting to know the characters. It takes skill to do both at the same time. That's what makes book worlds so fun. What's your favorite troupe? Mine is marriage of convivence."

She giggled; she'd never had a man ask her book type questions before. "Mine would be forced proximity, it has great dialogue in my opinion. But sprinkle in enemies to lovers and I'm sold."

He chuckled with her. "Oh, you like that sexual tension." He eyed her up and down. "Where are you from?"

"I was born in Florida, but I moved to Valdosta to live with my aunt when I was a kid. I've been in Atlanta six years now, so this has been my new home. I moved here with my ex-boyfriend." She shrugged. "I've always wanted to live here so we moved here together. What I didn't account for was him 'slipping' in some pussy after going out with his friends. I threw him out and I got a cat instead."

He frowned, "I'm sorry that happened. He must be stupid if he lost his chance with a woman like you. A cat woman that loves books? A woman after my own heart, I'm in love. Just kidding." He said awkwardly chucking and coughing, she smiled at his sudden nervousness. His nerd was showing, and it made him even sexier. "What kind of cat? What color is she? I love cats."

A man that loved cats? Her ex hated cats, that's why that was the first thing she did when his shit was finally out of her apartment. "Her name is Constance and she's black. I only like black things in my house." She said eying Calvin like she wanted every piece of him. He shifted in his seat, eying her back.

Before he could respond, Al came and placed her drink on the table. "Is there anything else I can get you?"

"Have you eaten?" Calvin asked her.

She pressed her lips together. "No, why?"

"Can you bring us an appetizer?" Calvin asked him. "It can be your choice, just nothing with dairy. I'll also have another whiskey sour. Also please add Ms. Gemini's tab to mine." She looked at him and almost broke her neck.

"You don't have to do that really. I can pay for my own drinks."

He looked deep into her eyes. "I didn't say you couldn't. Can I do something nice for the kind woman I'm having a great conversation with?" *Something nice? From a man?* He must want some pussy and she just might give it to him.

"I guess," she said with a shrug. When Al walked away, Calvin was back to looking through her soul and now soaked panties. "What is your idea of fun Mr. Cal? Do you enjoy bars often for women?" She asked eying him again, trying to not think about what he would taste like.

"I'm more of a silent reading party kind of guy. My friend suggested this bar, so this is my first time here. Then when I walked in, I saw a beautiful black woman with a book under her nose and I was caught up immediately. I knew I just had to wait for her to look up at me."

She threw her braids over her shoulder. "Oh okay. Well, I'm glad you were patient and didn't interrupt me," she said chuckling.

"Yea I always want to be respectful Gemini. My mother raised a gentleman." She hummed to herself. Even how her name sounded on his lips got her going. She picked up her drink and glanced at him as she took a cold sip.

"So, you actually get invited to silent reading parties? I've never been to one. Every time I find it. I'm a day late and a dollar short. Is it as relaxing as I think it is?"

Calvin nodded sipping his drink. "I prefer to host them at my library. It's just a group of people enjoying themselves with free resources the way it should be. That's why I love libraries. My family is in a different business, but I'm glad I found books."

Her eyebrows raised, "Oh what business?"

He scratched his chin and looked away; hesitation was in his eye. "They work in finance, but it wasn't my calling. I chose the route that makes the happiest, rather than the most money."

She nodded her head. She completely understood putting your happiness first. Her breakup allowed her to spend more time on herself, maybe more than she wanted. But she was more secure in what she wanted out of life. "I get that. My aunt didn't go to college, so she always encouraged me to climb the corporate ladder and that's what I've been doing. Sometimes I wish I made different choices but the choices I made led me to this moment so I'm not too upset."

"Yea I can't regret my choices when I get to sit this close to you."

"Stop making me blush," she said with a laugh. "You're giving me more attention than I deserve."

He gasped at her. "Do you not know how beautiful you are? I still can't take my eyes off of you. That yellow is poppin on your skin. I'm actually glad we came outside 'cause I saw a few guys look your way too and I don't like competitors. So, I had to move fast."

Hmm. He was watching her and everyone else around her. Al

came around the corner again with buffalo chicken tenders and Calvin's drink.

"Thank you, man. What should we toast to?" He asked looking towards Gemini.

She grabbed her glass and rose it towards him, "To getting out of our comfort zones and talking to people." His eyes gleamed as their glasses met. As they ate, they continued to talk about their favorite books of the year so far, book tracking apps, the authors they would like to meet and an intense match of fuck, marry, kill book character edition.

Gemini lost track of the words and got stuck on the sound of his warm voice. They unconsciously kept scooting closer to each other. Gemini would punch Calvin's shoulder if he made her laugh too hard. His hand found its way to rest on her thigh. When he would occasionally squeeze her leg, that was the confirmation she needed. "I'm just saying Gem, you should order a different drink. Maybe try something new?"

She scoffed. "No, I stick to what I know, and this is that. I know how it's supposed to taste and how drunk I get." They laughed louder. "I just have to say, you looked good from across the room. Like, more than good, like absolutely delicious. But our conversations have definitely made you even more attractive. Are you dating anyone?" She searched his eyes for hesitation.

He shook his head. "I'm single. You're the first person I've approached in a long time."

"Do you want to fuck me?" She asked leaning closer to him, only inches away from his face. Her fingertips brushing on top of his.

"I wouldn't be mad about it, but I ain't forcing." His milky voice made her shiver. He licked his lips while glancing at hers.

She hooked her index finger under his chin and pulled him in. When their lips met, they both immediately relaxed. Calvin leaned more into her mouth and she pulled his face closer. It had been so long since she kissed someone. They started slow, following each other's rhythm. His hand rested on the small of her back, gently squeezing her. While his other hand squeezed on her thigh, but not creeping up. It took everything in her to not get in his lap. She didn't know if he was showing as strong of restraint as her because he was so calm.

His lips were warm, and his breath tasted like whiskey. She wanted to lick the taste off his tongue. When her tongue brushed against his he moaned. They didn't care if anyone watched them. She rested her hand on the side of his face, her fingers resting on his sharp jaw line. She pulled back with a smile, but his was even wider. "So what are you trying to do?" He asked.

She leaned back and looked at him up and down. She saw his large print and wanted him in her mouth. "Close out the tab, meet me in my car." Her mouth began to water as her lips were still tingling from the kiss.

He immediately stood up, "I'll go do that. Which is your car?"

She stood up, all the blood rushing around her body. "It's the gold car at the end with the dark tint. See you in the backseat." She tried her best wink and walked to her car.

Was she the type of woman that gave blow jobs in bar parking lots? No. But she wanted to try something different for once. She didn't have to be in love to give him head, even if they did just meet.

Chapter Three

Calvin

How did Calvin get so lucky? Usually when he talked about books and other 'corny' things, he would immediately get shut down. Why did Gemini like him? He stood at the bar and waved down the bartender, Al. He did not want to keep her waiting. He quickly signed the receipt and walked outside.

Gemini's shape was beautiful. She was thick in all the right places. The way she sat on that bar stool made him want to grab a hand full of her ass right then. He wanted to be wrapped up in her braids. He needed her soft hands against his face again while he stroked her. But he was a gentleman, he'd wait for her to ask him to do it.

He wanted to pull her on his lap and suck on her breast on the patio. He didn't even care if people watched them. When her hand touched him, it was the ignition he needed, longed for. He grabbed the gold car handle and got in the backseat. As he sat down, she was putting her braids in a ponytail. *Am I about to get lucky again?*

She looked over at him. "Unbuckle your pants," she said

sternly. He quickly unbuckled his belt and zipped down his zipper. But he guessed he didn't move fast enough when she reached her hand in his boxers. His throat immediately got tight as her hand began massaging him. Her thumb gently brushing his head. A loud groan escaped from his throat. She leaned in close to him, "You like that baby?" She whispered in his ear.

"Yes fuck," he moaned and before he knew it, her warm mouth slid down his dick, her tongue slick. His eyes shot open as he rested his hand on the back of her head, wrapping her braids in his fingers. "Oh shit," she slurped and sucked better than he had ever experienced. Her lips squeezed his length, playing with his head with her tongue. Then deep throating all of him. He couldn't hold it anymore. He felt the rise, "Fuck I'm about to cum," he moaned. She shoved his dick to the back of her throat as he came.

He had to keep himself from screaming as he gripped the seat. *Where did this woman come from because she was not going to leave.* She easily swallowed and sat back up, wiping the corner of her mouth. He had no words, no thoughts.

"It's okay I'll wait for your voice to come back." She looked at him with a fire in her eyes that he wanted to be engulfed in.

"Damn Gemini, you didn't have to suck me like that."

She took her ponytail down, her auburn braids cascading around her body in the places he wanted to be. Even with the dark tint, he could see all of her. "Oh, I know. But trust me, I did it out of curiosity."

"Curiosity about what?" He said as he zipped his pants back up.

"How fast I could make you cum with my mouth, what you tasted like, what your cum tasted like." His jaw dropped.

"Well how do you feel now then?" He asked. "Now that you know."

"There is a hotel up the street. Want to meet there and have more fun? We can get a room?" She looked at him again with that same look. *Hunger.* Her body combined with the look she was giving him. He couldn't think. His post nut brain was too overwhelmed. How did the evening go from him taking a chance, to here? He needed to clear his mind since he had been drinking too.

"Um I want to, but we've both been drinking. We should probably sober up."

Her face fell. He said the wrong thing.

"It's only because we've been drinking. I don't want to take advantage or anything."

She threw her leg over him and sat on his lap. "Damn baby. I'm throwing neck and pussy at you and you're saying no? Why?" She leaned down and kissed him. He couldn't help but to feel down her back and squeeze her ass. How could he walk away now? As they kissed deeper and deeper, his hands crept up her thighs. Her lips quivered on his mouth. He had to be fair. His thumb started brushing on the outside of her seam. He could feel the heat coming from her sweet spot and loved it. He knew she was soaked as she rolled her hips on top of his hand.

He pulled back from kissing and looked at her. "You took care of me, so I'm going to do the same for you." He slowly laid her on her back on her center consol.

"What are you doing?" She laughed, moving her braids behind her.

"Do you want to take your pants off?" He asked her. She quickly slid her pants and panties off. As her legs extended next to his head, his mouth began to water at her glistening lips. He bent down and slowly licked her waterfall, flattening his tongue against her folds. She tasted so good, he needed and wanted more. She squealed as he dove in deeper, sucking her clit, penetrating her with his tongue. His face drenched with her sweetness.

Her nails lightly brushed his head as her legs shook. He looked up at her as she came on his face and mouth, watching her squirm and moan made him want to go even faster. He slid in his index finger and she groaned louder. She was so tight; the sound of her pussy made his mouth start to water again. He slid in a second finger and hooked them inside, her eyes rolled to the back of her head. Her thighs began to shake as she was about to cum again. Her couldn't wait until the clench of her was around his dick, but his fingers will have to do for now.

He slid in a third finger as her back arched, her hands on the drivers and passenger seat. He just noticed her head was starting to fall off the console. "Do you want me to stop?" He said looking down at her, slowly stroking her with his now soaked hand. His face glistening from her excitement.

She whined, "Did I say to fucking stop? Please don't I'm about to cum again."

"Bet," he bent back down and sucked on her clit, quickly

brushing his tongue against her rose. As she screamed, she squirted right on his face. Damn she was sexy; this couldn't be the last time he saw her.

"Oh my God," she said in between deep breaths. "Please don't get out of this car can we please go to a hotel tonight? I need some dick."

"No not tonight baby. But what's your number? We can next time," he said licking his fingers. She told him her number twice and he immediately texted her his name. "Trust me next time, you're gonna need time to stretch and brace yourself. I'll talk to you later." He opened the car door and looked around as he walked back to his car. The smell of her fresh on his upper lip and face. Would he regret walking away from her now? Yes. What if she was too pissed to ever talk to him again? What if she ignored him? What if she was an angel that didn't exist?

He had to wait until they were sober. He wanted to give her everything she needed and wanted.

Chapter Four

Gemini

What the fuck"! She screamed as she sat back up. How the fuck did he do that and just leave? He made her cum more than a few times with just his mouth and hand. She had to have more of him.

That was her new mission. A dildo does the job, but that mouth did wonders.

She did appreciate that he didn't want to take advantage of her. Her back and neck were definitely sore, but she hoped to see him again. When she looked down at her phone, she saw a number she didn't recognize with Calvin in the body of the message. She quickly saved his number as "Calvin Lips" because his lips did amazing things on her now drenched lips.

When Gemini finally made it home after going back into the bar for a cup of water and bathroom break, she drove home and took a hot shower, daydreaming of the man that stole her attention tonight. Constance, her cat, meowed at her as she stepped out of her grey titled shower. "Honey now is not the time to be talking crazy. I'm trying to not do a background check into this man." Constance meowed again and looked up at her, as Gemini walked past her in a towel.

With Gemini's day job being a Human Resources supervisor, she wore many hats. She helped with the call center, payroll reports, employment verification, interviews and training new staff. But she was sure to find out more about this mystery romance book loving man. She dried off, put on her old college sweatshirt, fed Constance, grabbed her laptop and blanket and dove on the couch. It was time to do some digging.

She sat with her legs crossed, her grey sticker covered laptop resting in front of her. She started doing general searches, 'Calvin Atlanta librarian' and a few others. Blank. Why didn't she get his last name? How was she supposed to find him? She started pacing her living room while Constance ate her wet cat food, unbothered by the immediate situation. Where was his digital footprint? What college did he go to? Did he say any of his friends names? She was on the case and she was going to solve it.

She grabbed a random notebook and began jotting general notes and questions down of what she could remember from their interaction...

No cheese on appetizer
Loves romance novels
Librarian
Family works In finance
Wiped her seat
GREAT long dick
FANTASTIC lips
Didn't want to fuck

She shook her head, she had to come back to reality before this man sucked her into a hole. Maybe that's what she wanted. Someone to help her escape the mundane cycle of going to work and coming home. She was so relaxed after her orgasms. Of course she masturbated at least three times a week, but being with a man made her feel warm again. It made her feel wanted. When she threw her notebook next to her laptop, her phone vibrated.

Calvin Lips: Hey Gemini, are you busy tomorrow night?

She dove at the couch and was quickly typing no.

WAIT.

You don't want to seem too too needy. She set an alarm for 3 minutes, she would respond then. She threw her phone down on the couch and walked the length of her apartment. While she was stress cleaning her bathroom mirror, the alarm yelled at her. She ran back to her phone and responded.

Gemini: Nope what's up?

Then an incoming Facetime came. Fuck *fuck*. People are supposed to ask before Facetiming! She was in her comfy clothes with no bra. She quickly turned her lamp on and jumped back on the couch trying to appear cool as she answered the phone.

"Hey, hey you!" she said too loudly cheesing on the screen, hoping her blanket pile wasn't showing in the background.

He chuckled, "Hey to you too. How are you? Did you make it home safe?" She zoned out as she looked at the screen. He was shirtless sitting on his bed, his back rested against a white wall. His upper body was more muscular and cut than she thought. The lines defined on his shoulders and chest made her mouth water as the shadows around the room danced on his body. She didn't want him to see her drool. She wondered what it would feel like to cuddle with him. *Stop yall just met, calm down.*

She looked around trying to play it off, "Yep I made it home. Here's what my spot looks like." She flipped her camera and showed her apartment living room. He nodded and smiled. His chain gleaming from the light above him.

"Wow your spot is beautiful. What's that on your laptop? Are you searching stuff on Google?" She slammed her laptop closed, kicked the notebook on the floor and flipped the camera back to her face.

"Oh nothing just... just researching.... something." She looked at her floor and back at the camera.

He arched his eyebrow at her, "Something hmm? I know

what my name and job is. You were looking me up huh?"

Her face got hot. *Now he's gonna think I'm a stalker, no dick for me.* She began to stammer as she looked for something to keep her hands busy. "Umm uhh I don't know what to say. I'm obviously a creep. You probably don't even want to talk to me anymore so I'll just hang up." She was about to the press the red button and hide under her bed.

"Why are you putting words in my mouth Gemini? I don't think it's weird." Her face softened as she looked up at the screen again. When she heard him say her name, it made her feel warm again. "In all honesty I was doing the same thing about you." He was looking into her too?

"Oh really? Did you find what you were looking for about me?" She bit her lip, looking into the camera at him.

He took a deep breath; his chest rose and fell still looking at her eyes through the screen with the same inquisitive look. His eyes made her melt in more places than one. "Nah, what I'm looking for is on this screen looking back at me… I kinda regret walking away but that was also why I called. I didn't want to leave you hanging. I genuinely enjoyed our conversations and didn't want to rush anything tonight." He scratched the bottom of his chin, was he nervous about something?

He continued, "I want to treat you to dinner before going to a hotel tomorrow night, if you still wanted to do that. I want to keep getting to know you." He had a sincere look in his eye. She couldn't say no if she wanted to. His brown eyes on her phone screen made something in her stomach swell. Then the flashbacks of his tongue on her flooded her brain.

"Yes I would like that, I get the room and you get dinner? It honestly doesn't have to be anything fancy." She didn't care where dinner was, as long as she was the dessert.

He smiled his million dollar smile again, "I'll plan dinner for us and it will be somewhere nice. It is a date."

"It's a date," she said with a smile, he stared back at her, nodding his head. She began to slyly lean forwards so her cleavage peaked. The sweatshirt was oversized on her, and he had to know what he missed out on, "I heard the dessert after dinner will be sweet." She said brushing her hand against her breast.

A low growl came from Calvin and she liked it. "I know that dessert is sweet, that's why I need another bite" he licked his lips. "I'm better at showing you, rather than telling you."

"Good that means I'm not holding back when I throw this ass back. You know, I'm thick." She stuck her tongue out.

"Yes, I do know. Shit I couldn't help but to cum. That was the best head of my life."

She took a deep breath, grazing her neck with her fingertips as he watched her. "How about we get to know each other a little better by playing a game?"

He nodded his head, "Sure what game baby?"

She had to hold in her moan by the way baby rolled off his lips. The way he hummed it made her whole body vibrate. *Focus Gemini focus.* "Let's play 20 questions, you think of 10 and I think of 10. We fire the questions at each other back and forth."

"That's a bet, let me think," he said looking away.

"That's fine I'll start. How old are you? I realized I forgot to ask earlier. I assumed since we were in a bar that you're over 21."

He laughed with his chest, "I'm 28, I'll be 29 next year. How old are you?"

She tucked her braids behind her ear. "You're not supposed to ask the same question as me cheater. But I'm 28 too."

He nodded, "Sweet, I have to ask. Are you a Gemini?"

She couldn't hold in her laugh or eye roll, as he laughed. "Of course I am. My birthday is May 28th. But I'm a May Gemini so I'm not as crazy as a June Gemini, just more calculating." She winked at him.

"Calculating hmm?" He studied her face. "I'm a Gemini too, June 5th." She pressed her lips together as he laughed so hard his camera fell. "I- I'm sorry but the look on your face is hilarious."

She rolled her eyes as he cleared her throat. "Well at least our birthdays recently passed. Happy belated," she chuckled.

"Happy belated! Where's Constance?" Calvin asked.

She looked around the room and saw her napping in her cat tree. "The sweet little darling is sleeping. Do you want to see her?"

"I'd love to," Gemini stood up and flipped the camera to her sleeping black cat. Her head was falling off the side and her paws were tucked into her fur.

Gemini admired Constance, lightly petting her behind the ear. "She's the closest I want to get to a child. I love her so much."

He beamed at her, "That is so sweet. Pets are amazing, I've never had one, but I'd love a cat. They're so chill. I might sneak one in the library just because. Do you have any siblings?"

Gemini smacked her lips. "I don't actually. Only child syndrome. What about you?"

"I thought we couldn't ask the same question sweetheart," he said chuckling. "I have a younger and older sister."

She flipped him off, "I made the rules so they don't apply to me". She stuck out her tongue. "Are you still close with them?"

He stuck his tongue out at her. "Yea I see them every week at Sunday dinner. My mom still cooks for us and everything still. My family aka the Grant clan is from Atlanta, and we all still live here so were not too far from each other. My sisters are a trip, but I love them."

Gemini yawned, "I'm sorry I didn't mean to yawn while you were talking. That sounds really nice. I wish my aunt was closer, she still lives in Valdosta. It's not that far but she's the closest family I've got." She covered her mouth and yawned again.

"Oh, don't mind me sleepy head, I'm glad your aunt is at least in Georgia. We've had a long night, go ahead and go to bed."

"You don't tell me when I go to sleep mister. I go when I want to." She yawned again, covering her mouth as her eyes watered.

"Then I, *suggest*, that you go to bed then," he said with a light chuckle.

She nodded and rubbed her eyes, "Okay talk to you soon?"

His smile gleamed on the screen, "Talk to you tomorrow, good night baby." The call ended. Well, he called her, so he definitely seemed interested in her. But it could also be because she offered him a hot plate of pussy.

She sleepily brushed her teeth, oiled her scalp and put her braids in her bonnet. They weren't going to get frizzy on her watch. She's already had them a few weeks and they were going to stretch for at least two more months.

As she walked to her bedroom, Constance meowed at her feet, following her into the room and hopping onto the bed. "I know I didn't talk to you much today, I'm sorry." Constance walked across the bed and took her usual place against Gemini's stomach. She silently wished Calvin was behind her, with his arm wrapped around her waist. Maybe that day would come, when he would whisper good night in her ear as they dozed off to sleep. But if there was anything she was confident in. It was that she was going to fuck the shit out of him eventually

Chapter Five

Calvin

Calvin was mindlessly putting plastic covers on the recently donated books and labeling them. He decided to come into work on a Saturday, which was not too unusual for him. He actually enjoyed being there. The walls of books and the smell of paper would keep him company. The silence in the walls felt good. If he stayed home, his arm would eventually get tired and he would've paced his townhome until he started getting ready for his date. He was so nervous and excited about tonight. The noise of the plastic and the repetitive movement of placing stickers and barcodes had become ASMR for him. He preferred to be surrounded by books anyway so his mind would be at peace.

Gemini's taste was still in the corner of his mouth. He couldn't wait to treat her to dinner and hopefully get desert. He called three different restaurants this morning to make reservations, just in case if she didn't like his favorite. He already texted her good morning and wished she had a good day, she responded and wished him the same.

Calvin: Do you have any allergies?

Gemini: Nope

Calvin: Anything you don't have a taste for?

Gemini: Uhh no seafood boil. I eat crabs too messy and I don't want you to see that side of me lol are you going to give me a hint? Just tell me where were going

Calvin: Nope you have to be patient lol just look great. Even though that won't take much

Gemini: Noted 😄

He looked up at the ceiling. It still looked the same from when he was a kid, creamy white with dark wood beams surrounding each corner. The main librarian always helped him with any and all questions he had. He saw librarians as master researchers and always wanted to be one. No matter how random the topic, she could find a book about it. He continued to visit her even after he came back from college. He had to pay it forward when the library was going to close. The isles and bean bag chairs held too many stories and adventures of his childhood. He made friends, traded books, and listened to great CDs. The library needed a private owner that cared about people and the pursuit of knowledge and cultures.

Now, the walls had a fresh coat of paint and they got some great pieces of furniture from a Hotel outlet store he found an hour away. The artwork was donated from local black artists. He even created a piece, but it was hidden in plain sight. He rarely showed people his artwork but a piece of him had to hang on the walls. No one has been able to guess which painting is his yet, not even Greg.

Last year, some parents began complaining because the library still had banned books available for checkout. The protests went all the way to the mayor's office. Calvin knew he was the best person to run it. He just graduated with a Masters in Library Science and knew exactly how to take the library to the next level. After a call to some investors, including his mother, he was able to keep it open and co-own it with Greg. Even though libraries don't return a huge profit, he doesn't regret it. Hearing a group of kids talk about their favorite books was his motivation. Black people weren't always offered the opportunity to even read. To be a black owned library filled Calvin with pride because he's able to promote local black authors, share historical information and give recommendations on a variety of topics.

But his family's business had a much faster pace.

He tells people that his family works in finance, but the family business is more complicated. It started about 30 years ago when his mother was working in one of the most popular strip clubs in Atlanta. Yes strip club, she was a dancer. One of the best they had, when she tells the story. She saved her money and purchased the club she worked in. At only 24 years old, after graduating with a business degree, she doubled the income of everyone there with a few cosmetic and business changes. When she became pregnant with his older sister, Coraline, at 25 she decided to focus more on the business side of operations. She went back to school for her MBA while being a business owner and single mother.

Now, Mama was 54 and the CEO of Grant Enterprises with locations in 15 different states across the country. His big sister Coraline was Vice President and his baby sister, Casey, was the Executive Training director. He was grateful for the financial wealth of his family, but he still never wanted to get involved with the family business. His family was extroverted and enjoyed hosting big parties with huge waves of people coming in every hour, women hanging and dancing from the ceiling. Even though all of the clubs were ethical and legal, they weren't his scene. He preferred to hide in the library and pretend he didn't exist. His phone vibrating in his pocket brought his attention back.

Mama: Good morning favorite son! Coming for dinner Sunday?

Calvin: I'm your only son lol and of course. Wouldn't miss it

He began thinking about the possibilities of the Sunday dinner menu. Would she make pot roast? Black eyed peas and rice? Her famous sweet potato pie? His stomach began to growl and he wasn't even hungry. He always appreciated his Mama's cooking. When he was a kid, he would cook dinner with her, on the rare occasions she was home at night.

When her hours became steadier after having Casey, Sunday dinners became our ritual to regroup with the family. *Should I mention Gemini to them?* No, it's only been a day, literally. It would depend on how dinner went tonight.

When he made it home from work, he lit the candle in his bathroom and turned on the shower. As he looked at himself in the mirror, he could see the hesitation in his own eyes. He took a deep breath and said, "You are worthy, capable and acceptable. You are amazing and loving." He took another deep breath and walked into his standing shower.

Calvin pulled into Gemini's apartment complex and sat in the parking lot. He had on his favorite black button-down shirt with tailored grey dress pants. He couldn't anticipate what she would be wearing. When she stepped outside, her spaghetti strap black dress hugged her in the places he wanted to explore. Even though it was dark outside, the street lights lit her beauty just enough. His mouth watered reminiscing about how good she tasted, he tried to not think if she was wearing a thong or not because his dick would get hard immediately. He hoped to swim in her skin tonight, but just being in her presence was nice too.

He noticed he was still sitting in the driver seat as she got closer, looking around the parking lot. *Move man move.* As she walked up to the car, he hurriedly got out and opened the car door for her. Not that he practiced how to hold the door for her or anything. *Okay maybe I did, don't judge.* "Good evening Gem," Calvin said with a charming smile.

She smiled back and yanked his heart strings, "Hi, good

evening." She outstretched her arm and gave him a hug. Her silky alto voice brushed his ear. Her sweet perfume teased his nose, not quite floral but sugary. She had on light make up and mascara. Her lip gloss shined under the street light. He watched her head as she got into the car, closing the door behind her. He just noticed that her dress was open back and it made his dick jump in anticipation. She looked so smooth and edible. He was determined to make sure tonight was perfect. This woman was too perfect to mess up.

When they arrived at the restaurant, he parked and opened the door for her again. He offered his hand to her as she stepped out. "Calvin, you have to stop being so sweet to me. I'm not used to guys holding doors open for me and shit, I can get it myself."

He gasped in a sarcastic way. "Never! I won't stop as long as you're close to me." She half smiled while looking away from him. He saw a gleam in Gemini's eye that made him want to pull her in and kiss her. But he was going to be patient and not rush her into anything. The restaurant was New Orleans themed, and the rich smell of yellow rice, gumbo and fresh beignets met them as they swung the door open. He swore he heard Gemini's stomach growl. Calvin approached the greeter, "Good evening. I have reservation under Calvin Grant."

The woman looked at her tablet and made a few taps. "I see," she grabbed the menus, "Follow me please." He grabbed Gemini's hand and followed her to the table, he could feel her reluctance in his grasp. The table was just small enough to be intimate and have space for plates. He pulled out Gemini's seat and sat across from her. "Your server will be with you shortly."

She placed the menus down in front of them and walked away.

Calvin never realized when he was staring at Gemini. He couldn't help it. He felt so blessed. Even if she asked him to take her straight home, he wouldn't mind. He knew he had the best view and wasn't ready to let it go yet. "You love looking at me like that don't you?" She asked matching his gaze.

He gave her an inquisitive look, "Like what?"

She shrugged, "Like I'm special or something." She started looking away, rubbing on her arms. Was she uncomfortable? Cold?

He reached across the table and grabbed her hand, rubbing the top of her knuckles. "You are special. I'm glad we're out together again."

She half smiled, "Me too. I guess I'm still a little nervous. You're not gonna kill me right? I'm too cute to kill?"

He kissed her hand. "I could never raise my hand at you. You are too beautiful to butcher." They laughed as she pulled her hand back.

"Do you mind if we take a selfie to send to my friend Serena? We always do that when we go out with new people."

Calvin grinned, "No I don't mind." Gemini took out her phone as Calvin leaned forward on the table. His adorable smile caught in the flash.

She showed him the photo. "I just realized were matching with our black. How cute?" He winked at her.

The server came and asked for their drink order. Gemini

asked for a Sprite and Calvin got a water. "Wow, a water? You don't want anything stronger?"

He shook his head maintaining her eye contact, "No, I want to stay hydrated for what the future might bring." He looked her up and down.

"Might bring? The room reservation is made honey. I had too much fun yesterday." She took a sip, maintaining his eye contact.

He exhaled as he picked up the menu. "Good," he bit his bottom lip and licked it, remembering her sweet taste on his tongue. The anticipation of wanting to be inside her was growing more and more. It made his dick swell under the table. *Patience tiger.* She reviewed her menu. When the server returned, they both got jambalaya. The room was filled with multiple different conversations, but at their table it was just them. The restful silence filled them. He grabbed her hand and rubbed his thumb on her palm. She pulled her hand back.

"I'm sorry." She rested her hand on the table next to her silverware.

He put his hands on his lap, "Sorry I don't mean to do too much. I like touching you. I can't explain it but I like how you feel."

"No, I'm sorry." She rubbed her neck and bit her index finger. "I'm not super used to PDA. This is my first date in a long time so I'm just...yea. I'm usually more touchy feely when I've been drinking."

He nodded as he sat back in his chair, "Your comfort is what's most important to me Gem. I didn't mean to cross a line." He rubbed his hands on his lap.

"It's okay," she said looking away. Now the silence between them was awkward. He was trying not to beat himself up about it, but how could he not? She radiated confidence and control. He wanted to know everything about her. What were the thoughts that passed her mind? What was she thinking about now?

He cleared his throat and she looked at him again. Their brown eyes studying each other. Everything was silent for a few seconds as he tried to read the detail in her face. Her round eyes, her glistening lips and kissable nose. *Okay now say something Calvin.* "So, since you fell asleep during 20 questions last night, can we keep playing?"

She chuckled. "Shut up! Yea we can keep playing." She thought for a moment. "If this is too personal of a question just let me know, but what is your sexuality?"

He gulped, fixing his glasses on his nose. She came out swinging. Should he answer the question truthfully or just tell her he's straight? He had a feeling that if he told the truth, Gem would want to leave. But he didn't want to start something nice with a lie out of fear. He already lied about his family business. "Oh uh that's not too personal… Well honestly I'm bisexual." He twirled his thumbs. "I've never been with a man, but I want to. I know I'm not straight."

Her eyebrows raised as she took another sip, "Thank you for feeling comfortable enough to tell m-"

He couldn't even hear to what she said, every time he mentioned his sexuality the vibe always changed. "Yea, if you want to leave, we can just get our food to go." He stood up and she stayed sitting down.

"Why do we need to leave? Is something wrong?" She looked at him with concerned eyes. Did he miss something?

He sat back down, "You don't want to leave?"

"No, I don't, at least not yet. I asked if you wanted to talk about it. I still want to continue the evening. I've been having fun so far." He was confused, but she continued. "I don't care that you're bi. I'm bi-curious myself. But I'm terrified to approach a woman and nobody wants a baby gay. So here I am." She shrugged. "I don't judge people cause I wouldn't want someone to judge me. The people that are quickest to judge, are the ones that can't handle the mirror. I always appreciate honesty over lying."

Calvin exhaled deeply, "I don't know why it's such a taboo topic."

"Me either." She opened her hand for his on the table. He looked at her hand hesitantly. *Now she wants to hold my hand?* She extended and wiggled her fingers and smiled the way that made Calvin's stomach tumble and dick stiffen. "Come on, I won't pull away this time. I miss touching you too. Sorry I pulled away earlier, I unfortunately do that a lot. It's a reflex." He joined his hand with hers and half smiled. She drew circles in the palm of his hand. The electricity dancing around their palms.

"Nobody is a 100% perfect. I won't judge you when you pull away, I'll be patient," he said with a grin as he brought her hand to his mouth and kissed her knuckles, then her palm, then her wrist. From the look of her cheeks, she was definitely blushing. Was she starting to sweat?

"Come on, it's your turn to ask a question," she said breathlessly.

He chuckled; she was right. His thumb continued dancing around her hand. "What's your favorite snack?"

She looked around the restaurant and leaned forward, resting her other hand under her chin. He leaned forward too. He focused on the intensity of her eyes looking back at him. "Don't judge me, but I like to eat Jolly Ranchers and Hot Fries."

His face scrunched up, "Like, together?" He couldn't hold in his laugh.

"See, I knew you would make that face. Yes, I'm weird. I like to eat sweet and spicy snacks together. Have you never eaten a sugar donut with hot wings? The sweet and savory tastes are amazing."

He pressed his lips together, "No, I haven't, but I'll take your word for it." She hit his arm as she laughed. That one kinda hurt, she'd have to pay for that hit later. "Your turn miss."

She wiggled her nose in the cutest way as she thought of a question. "What did you go to school for?"

Calvin brushed off his shoulders in the corniest way he could, "I have my bachelor's and master's in Library Sciences."

Gemini applauded with the tips of her fingers and pursed her lips, "Oh my, in library sciences. I didn't know it was a science. Congratulations! We love seeing educated black men."

"Yea, the library is an important piece of the community. So, I'm glad to be working in the same library I would visit as a kid. It still has a special spot in my heart. Did you go to school?

She smiled. "Mmhm I have my Bachelors in Business Management."

He smiled even wider, "Okay miss degreed. How long have you been into reading?" He stared at her as she thought about it. Her braids were half up, half down and it brought even more attention to her stunning face.

"You know, I've been reading for a while actually. My aunt would take me with her to the library and it always seemed like the most amazing place. I loved when a random puppet show came into town. I still feel like that kid sitting on that carpet. I listened to so many good albums there too. I listened to Usher's and Beyonce's whole discography. Reading also helped me stay out of trouble. Kids don't want to mess with the new girl reading in the corner."

Calvin's eyebrow raised, "Beyonce? Are you apart of the Bey hive? Yes, it counts as a question."

She laughed, "I'm not getting people fired from their jobs but she's one of the greatest entertainers of our time. I mean have you even listened to Renaissance?"

He nodded, "Yes, I have. It's really good." She pressed her lips together in a line.

"Really good? It is fabulous, it is perfect. Will I ever stop listening to it? Probably not. It's a masterpiece. She did what needed to be done."

When their orders came, they ate and giggled so much that the tables around them started to look. He enjoyed listening to her music choices, her childhood with her aunt. Calvin didn't care if people glanced at them for having a good time, let them look. Gemini was hands down the most beautiful woman in the room. Her glowing rich coffee skin, the way her lips pursed when she took the first bite of her food.

"Oh my," she said with a sigh. "This is the best jambalaya I've had since I was a kid. My aunt used to make this all the time." She scooped another spoonful. "I can trust your food recommendations now. If the food was horrible, I would've hesitated with the sex."

"I'm glad, I am picky when it comes to certain things. Especially my food and what I surround myself with." She blushed as she looked back down at her plate. It was the small movements she made that he noticed. How she held her fork, the way she patted the corners of her mouth with her napkin. He wanted to take care of her, even though she didn't need it. When the check came, he paid for dinner before her hand reached into her black Telfar purse.

"Oh, you didn't want to go 50/50?" She asked.

"No," he said putting his wallet back in his pocket. "This is a date and what we agreed to yesterday." She grabbed her wallet.

"Mmm I'm paying the tip." She chuckled as she set the $20 on the table.

Calvin grumbled, "Yea, you're getting more than the tip tonight."

When they walked out, her arm was looped into his as he held every door open for her. Calvin's heart warmed feeling her weight in his arm. He didn't want to let go when they made it to his car. But he grabbed the door handle anyway and held the door for her once again. The view he got when she sat down, he'd open any and all doors for her. Even the one to his heart. When he got in the driver's seat, he turned and asked her, "Anywhere else you want to go?"

Chapter Six

Gemini

Calvin looked at her with expecting eyes. The night was going amazing. She hadn't laughed this much in too long. The food was genuinely amazing. If she said she wanted to go home, would he be cold towards her? *Bitch you know damn well you want his dark chocolate ass.* Why starve herself? She had a craving she had to get her hands on. "I mean I still want to go to the hotel. If you're cool with that?"

He smiled. "Yes, I'm still cool with that. I just didn't want to force you if you changed your mind. Do you want to make any stops beforehand?"

She looked out the window, "I'm craving something sweet. Want to get a milkshake?"

He started the car, "I can't have milkshakes. But I'd love to take you."

"I'm sorry I forgot. We don't have to go then."

He put his hand on her seat as he looked out the back window to back up. His cologne brushed across her nose and she was happy yet again. "It's okay, Cook Out isn't far. Let's get you milkshake." She couldn't hold in her squeal. She texted him the hotel address while they were in the drive thru to put it into the GPS. "Awesome it's only 15 minutes away," Calvin said with a slick smile on his face.

She decided to get a Peach Cobbler Milkshake. It was so thick that her straw immediately got stuck. "It must be good I see." He said with a low chuckle.

Her ankles were crossed as she slurped the milkshake. "Yes, don't judge me." This had to be the best tasting thing. He made a left turn, but the lid wasn't on all the way. The milkshake spilled on his shirt, cascading peaches and ice cream on him and his car seat. "OH MY GOD I am so sorry. Fuck why did I have to want a milkshake." He opened his center counsel and grabbed some napkins.

"It's okay it wasn't your fault. It'll come out. I'll just have to take a shower when we get to the room. Oh, it's going down my pants." She couldn't hold in her laugh because of the way his face twisted from the cold cascading down his body while he drove. His hands clenched the steering wheel. "This is so ironic," he started with a low slow laugh that grew along with hers. They pulled into the hotel parking lot.

"I am so so so sorry again, Calvin," she said, taking off her seat belt.

"Stop apologizing, it's okay." When they pulled into a spot, he started to unbutton his top and put it to the side. She couldn't take her eyes off of his chest. The way the lines on his body met. She didn't see one tattoo, but a few curls of black chest hair. She wanted to spread the milkshake across his nipples and lick it off. Yes, she had to devour him tonight, if not just to scratch the itch. He grabbed a hoodie from the backseat and put it on. *Booo.* "Do you have to check in?"

"Not in person." She shook her phone. "I've got a key on my phone, but I can pick up a physical key for you at the front desk." She opened her door and got out.

"Sounds like a plan." He followed her to get the key and up to the room. When they walked in, the king bed was in the center. A desk was off to the side with a TV that probably wouldn't get turned on. "I'm going to take a shower real quick." He leaned and kissed her cheek. Her whole body seemed to vibrate as her heart thumped at double speed. He quickly threw his hoodie off as he made his way to the bathroom. His affection felt so real, like he meant every kiss. It was hard to not like PDA when Calvin's lips felt so good on her skin. She began playing music so the room wouldn't feel so empty as she waited. Should she keep her dress on or take it off and pose on the bed? Should she get naked and lay in the sheets? Gemini was surprised by how nervous she was all of a sudden for her own idea.

Then Calvin stepped out of the shower, naked. Her throat became dry. His dark skin gleamed of shower water and gold. His strong shoulders, cut chest, the curly trail that began at his naval was still wet. She didn't feel so bad about spilling the drink on him now. Especially since it meant that she got to see him naked sooner. "Like what you see?" Calvin said eying her up and down, spinning in a circle. His muscular body shining. Even his back was cut. His ass was still glistening. She couldn't wait to get her hands on him.

She nodded her head and bit her bottom lip, "Fuck yes, come over here. I don't care if you haven't dried off yet."

He slowly walked over to the bed. She watched his every step. Brown Skin by India.Arie began playing. He leaned over her, his arms on either side. She looked at his round lips and up at him, a grin on his face. His chain dangled in front of her, just barely brushing her chest. When they made eye contact, it felt like slow motion. She grabbed his chin and pulled him into a kiss. It wasn't fast or rushed, but passionate. Her hands couldn't cover enough of him. As they kissed deeper, he picked her up and placed her by the pillows. She brushed her hands down his neck, shoulders and chest. He moaned into her mouth as she drew circles on his nipples.

Hearing his breaths increase, made her even more confident. She rubbed her hands up and down his back, lightly kissing his neck and shoulder. Seeing Calvin squirm just from the slightest touch made her want more, crave more. This dress needed to come off right now. She tried to hike her dress over her head, but her braids got tangled. "What are you rushing for baby? Let me." He slowly untangled her braids and threw the dress to the side of the bed. She watched him pause as he admired her body. Her bra and burgundy thong exposed. He froze with his mouth agape.

"Like what you see?" she said teasingly. She brushed her big toe up his leg. The way his eyes danced around her body made her fuzzy.

Their eyes met again. "You are so perfect. I want to lick you," he whispered. Her body quivered under him. He bent down, and lightly kissed her shoulder, color bone, unhooking her bra as he kissed the gap between her breast. Her bra dropping to the floor without a sound.

She couldn't help but lay her head back, she had to enjoy this. He forced her to be in the moment and she was enjoying it. He was so slow, intense with each move that it made her focus on receiving the pleasure. It was intoxicating and teasing. He slowly hooked his hand in between her love handles and thong as he slid them off of her in one smooth move.

She wrapped her legs around his waist and pulled him into her, his dick rested on the outside of her lips. "Fuck me please, don't make me beg. But I will."

"Oh, you're begging already sweetheart, but you're still not ready yet." His brown eyes pierced her as he bent down and blew on her folds. It sent shivers and goosebumps up her spine. He began with a slow lick with circles on her clit then devoured her. She gasped and grabbed the back of his head. Her toes cracked and curled with each tongue flick. "Your pussy is so fucking tasty baby," he mumbled. When he slid both of his fingers in, she rolled her neck. Her whole body felt like it was filled with light as he stroked her. "You're finishing more than once tonight damnit. Cum on my fingers."

He twisted and turned his fingers while sucking and applying the perfect pressure. She couldn't hold it in if she tried. She screamed as she grinded his face. The explosion in her mind and body made her teeth chatter. A part of her wanted him to fuck her into oblivion another never wanted his face to move. Her back arched as her second rise came again, catching her by surprise. She groaned, "Please fuck me already baby I'm so turned on... *fuck*."

The corner of his lips lifted and kissed her thigh as he rose up. "Since you've been a good girl." He hovered his face above hers, barely an inch away.

She kissed him again, licking his lips as he slid his thick 7-inch dick inside of her. He groaned in her ear and bit her ear lobe as she gasped. He filled all the space in her and more. Her arms wrapped around his back.

"Fuck," they said at the same time as Calvin stroked her. His hips rolling to the rhythm of the music. As he went deeper and deeper inside of her, the more she moaned and twitched against him. She couldn't stop staring at his chest, sweat was starting to glisten on his skin. He was hitting all the spots she needed him too. Her hands slowly went down and rested at his waist, her thumbs brushing his skin as his face tightened.

"I'm going to cum again," she whispered.

His eyes shot open, looking down at her. "Cum baby, I got you. Cum on your dick" he said breathlessly. He stared into her eyes like he meant it. She squeezed his ass as she screamed, he continued stroking her as she tightened and released. She felt like the bed was spinning. "Are you okay baby?" He asked concerned, slowly his pace.

"Yes! Please don't stop," she said in between gasps.

"Good girl," he whispered rolling his hips against hers. "I'm going to hit all your spots do you fucking hear me?" He turned her to the side, slowly lifting her leg.

"Fuck yes," she cried. She tightened around him as her legs shook. He didn't stop. He kept looking down at her with passion and strength in his burning eyes. She grabbed the sheets under her to keep her steady. He grabbed her hands and put them on his forearms, "Grab me, quit grabbing those sheets. They haven't even earned it."

She quickly slapped her hands on his arms and their connection grew more. Her hands massaging his muscular arms, digging her nails into him. Their energies combined. She's never experienced sex like that. They were on the same speed, tempo, plane, universe. Gemini swore she saw stars and the room glow as she came again. Her back arching, eyes squeezing shut, her mouth open. He bent down and kissed her lightly on her lips, sucking her top lip as she moaned in his mouth.

He leaned back, gently grabbing her ankles and crossing them. With her legs at a 90 degree angle, he entered her again and again. His arm tightening around her legs as he kissed her calf, down to her knee, licking the back of her knee. *Damn.* She moaned louder as she tossed her head further back into the pillow. The headboard creaked with each stroke but she ignored it. He smacked her ass. "Turn around," he said with a growl. She slowly rolled onto her stomach and put a pillow under her pelvis.

He smacked her ass again and kissed her lower back. "You are so beautiful sweetheart. Are you ready for me?"

"Yes baby," she said with an exhausted sigh.

He squeezed her ass, spread her lips and settled inside of her. When she screamed, he went faster as his cold sweat lightly landed on her back. His hands squeezed her waist, his thumb brushing up her spine. He arched her back more as he continued, her muffed moans dimmed by the pillows.

She begged, "Choke me, please." He leaned forward and grabbed the front of her neck, not missing a stroke. She instantly tightened around him more as he began whispering in her ear.

"I love watching you take this dick. I told you I'm better at showing you, than telling you. Are you going to keep taking it?"

She gasped as he pounded harder, "Yes sir." He licked the back of her ear and she bit into the mattress.

"Nah, I want to look at you, pick up your face." She lifted her head, "Good girl. You're my good girl." He took his hand off her neck and dug his nails into her ass, slowly stroking her from the side. She screamed and clenched. "You okay?" he asked.

"Fuck yes! Don't stop."

He began to slow down, and she sat back on her knees keeping balance on her hands, twerking on his hard length as he entered her. "Damn I love this," he groaned. "Keep shaking that fucking ass." She threw her ass in a circle and bounced it up and down. He couldn't even move. She sat back, her ass against his stomach, her braids swinging around her. She knew she looked as amazing as she felt.

In this moment, she didn't care if Calvin never talked to her again. But she was enjoying this moment with him. *Maybe it could be like this forever?* He grabbed her waist flush against him. She yelped from how deep he was. He slowed his pace but had more intention with his stroke, breaking all her walls with nothing but focus and determination in his eyes. "Are you ready baby?" He said as another drop of his sweat landed on her back. She shivered.

"I'm ready for anything baby, I'm yours." He growled and squeezed her hips tighter as he went faster. His sweat flying off him. Gemini's body went limp, falling forward with her ass in the air. Her face was buried in the pillows as he spread her lips and sucked her clit. He licked her rim as she gasped.

He slowly lifted her legs. Her ass and legs hung in the air as he continued to devour her. Gemini's mind couldn't focus as she came on his face. *Damn he's doing something to me, shit.* He slowly placed her legs back down, kissing her slowly up her back as he put it back in. The sound of him entering her seemed to bounce off the walls. She never wanted him to stop.

He pressed his thumb against her asshole, her bottom lip quivering. Her legs and body shook in response. "Choke me," she moaned to him.

He grabbed the back of her neck, squeezing his fingers against the side of her neck as he shoved deeper inside of her. She quivered under him, thankful that they met. "Fuck I'm about to cum," Calvin said breathing heavy. She quickly turned around and covered his dick with her mouth. By the time she pushed him deeper down her throat, he came, gripping the back of her head as he gasped and groaned. She swallowed, wiping her mouth as she sat up. Even though she was on birth control, she liked how he tasted.

He threw himself down on the bed. "Shit, you swallowed again? You're d- doing something to me, damn."

She slowly got up from the bed, "You did your work and I had to do mine baby. You were fucking me like you had something to prove." She limped to the bathroom and rinsed her mouth. Even though she didn't mind the taste of him, she still wanted to wash it down. When she walked back to the bedroom, he had his arms behind his head, his dick still hard as a rock, looking at her like she was a glowing African goddess. She got back into bed with him and laid her head on his shoulder, nestling her forehead against his neck. "Do you want to go another round?" she asked brushing her fingers against his chest.

He smiled as he lifted her chin to his mouth. Their heads turned as they kissed. She licked his lips and he groaned leaning into her more. His tongue dancing in her mouth, her hand squeezing his ass. Then he ducked his head under the covers. She couldn't move if she wanted to. His hands pulled her waist into his mouth, with the way he sucked her clit and held her down, she was where she was supposed to be. When he came up for air, she was out of breath, her hand rested on her forehead. He climbed on top of her, "Do you still want more baby?" He kissed her cheek, then down her jaw line.

She moaned as her arms rested on his shoulder, looking at him deep into his eyes. "Yes, I do," she said breathlessly. He entered her again, as her nails brushed against the back of his neck. His hands holding her neck, his fingers playing in her braids.

The way he groaned in her ear made her roll her hips against him more. She moaned and bit his top lip. His rhythm perfect against hers. He kept giving her what she wanted, him. There was no sense of time. Nothing moved around them. Their skin hot against each other's as they licked and bit each other for hours, making their mark on each other forever.

This was her favorite part of the story.

GASP. Gemini sat up, shocked out of her sleep. Her skin was clammy, her neck was tight and her heart was racing. *Where am I? A dream? Where am I?* Her breathing kept getting faster and faster. *Oh no, I have to get out of here.* She couldn't have Calvin see her like this, drenched in sweat, confused and shaking. She took a slow deep breath trying to calm down as she ran the events over in her head. They went to dinner, then came here and fucked the shit out of each other. Calvin. She glanced down at him. *He's still here?* Calvin was sound asleep next to her, on his stomach, cuddled under the comforter. He was still naked, the moonlight from the window poured onto his face. This was not what she had planned.

She had to get out of there.

They just met yesterday; they couldn't share a bed together. She had sworn off men. Where did that lead her? The most amazing sex she'd ever had in her life. It would ruin everything if he saw her in shambles like this. She was supposed to be strong, not shaking because a random anxiety attack hit her. No more cuddling, no more lovey dovey. Only couples cuddle and love up on each other through the night.

She slowly got out to bed and went to the bathroom. She splashed some cold water on her face, which helped even more with bringing her back to reality. When she came back out, she quickly got dressed, grabbed her purse and headed for the door. She looked at Calvin again before she left. His chest rising and falling as he slept. His arm stretched out across her pillow.

She didn't have to leave right now. She could stay and cuddle more, it wouldn't kill her. It had been a while since she stayed the night with someone, anyone. She took a step towards the bed. He moved in the sheets. No, he probably just wanted the sex anyway. *Why would he want me to stay?*

She turned around and grabbed the door handle without a second thought. She quietly closed the door behind her. As she made her way to the lobby, she tried to get a car service. Turns out, most businesses are closed at 3:00am. She put in as many requests as she could, rubbing her forehead as she sat in the empty lobby. Maybe she should've stayed in the room.

Calvin Lips: You didn't have to leave

She blew out air. Then her phone pinged, *Ride 3 minutes away*.

Chapter Seven

Calvin

Click. "Did the door just close?" Calvin slowly opened his eyes and brushed his hand across the bed. *Empty*. He sat up slowly and rubbed his eyes. *She left?* She didn't have to leave. The smell of her hair oil lingered on her pillows. He missed the feel of her. Her skin, her lips, her hair. He didn't expect her to leave like this. That was why they went to dinner then came here, he still wanted to spend time with her. He thought it was a real date. If he just wanted to fuck, he would've just paid for the room himself and not planned a dinner. He couldn't lose her, not with knowing more about her. He grabbed his phone and texted her. Her response came seconds later.

Gemini: Good night Calvin

Calvin: I'll leave, you can stay

He started getting dressed. There's no way she was gone already, maybe he could catch her and convince her to stay. She shouldn't have to pay for a ride, she paid for the room. She could've woken him up, he would've driven her home himself. He searched and put his pants, hoodie and glasses on while slipping his wallet and hotel key in his pocket. He swung open the door and started running down the hallway. He had to catch her.

He ran down the few flights of stairs, pushed open the door and looked out into the lobby, empty. He ran out of the hotel doors outside, the warm air met his face. Then he saw *her*. She was opening the car door and glanced at him. Time stopped for 3 seconds as they made eye contact. She still looked beautiful in the black dress, but her braids were completely down. The red wall back around her, covering the space around her. The braids he ran his hand through. He reached his hand out towards her and took a step. She flinched, then looked down and got in the car.

He stood there at the hotel entrance as she rode away. *How could she leave me like this?* She didn't promise him that she would stay. But after dinner, he thought she would. Maybe he should've headed the warning she gave him about pulling away. He rubbed his head and walked back into the hotel. The front desk attendant gave him a curious look. He approached the counter. "I would like to add my payment information to room 346."

She began typing on the computer, her gum popping while her nails typed. "May I see the card please?"

He handed his card over. The least he could do was pay for the room since *she* wasn't going to stay in it. The attendant handed him his card back and a receipt. "Have a good night," he said with a nod as he returned to the room. He gathered all of his things and made sure that *she* didn't leave anything either. What was the point? Would she even want to see him again? He thought he did a good job. She definitely seemed satisfied. Even he lost track of how many times she came. He was confused about everything. He did what he was supposed to do. Why couldn't he have her?

As soon as he kicked his shoes off at home, he laid his head down. Then he cursed himself for not bringing the pillowcase she slept on. It would've been weird, yes. But at least he could smell *her* scent. "Fuck, I like her. I've known her a day and I like her." He rubbed his forehead until he soothed himself to sleep.

The sun burning through his window woke him. It was Sunday, which meant family dinner. He grabbed his phone and began playing music as he stepped into his bathroom. After getting out of the shower, he said his mantra and began getting ready. Trying to not think about the way him and Gemini's eyes met his last night, the feel of her lips on his shoulder, or her teeth brushing against his arms. He rubbed his temples. He had to act like everything was okay or his sisters would sense it. Then the investigating would begin.

He pulled into the long winding driveway of his mother's place. But this six bedroom, eight bath house wasn't the one he grew up in. She now lived in a gated community in Cobb County. He still remembered the 2-bedroom apartment by the airport they used to live in. Casey, his youngest sister, had the privilege of only remembering 'the big house'. He and his sister used to share a room. But with Mama's college fund, he and his sister went to grad school with no debt. Even though they weren't broke as kids, they didn't have nearly as much money as they did now.

As he walked up to the door, he checked his clothes to make sure not a thing was out of place. He was wearing khaki shorts with a freshly ironed navy-blue shirt with some Sperry's. He remembered that he put on lotion when he stepped out of the shower, but he checked his ankles to make sure. He turned his key into the door. "Here we go again," he whispers to himself. The scent of fried chicken and collard greens graced his nose as the door swung open. The sound of laughter hit his ears.

"Hey I made it," he said sheepishly.

"Aww my little brother made it." His big sister Coraline appeared from out of the kitchen with a wide fake smile. She was the most business centered, but she didn't really have a choice. Someone had to follow Mama's footsteps. Coraline was wearing dark, blue jeans with a crisp blue stripped button-down top with the sleeves folded to her elbows. She was 6 feet tall, so she was a few inches taller than Calvin. Her freshly permed dark brown hair bounced and swayed at her shoulders as she hugged him. "How are things in that *little* book world of yours? Keeping you too busy to attend the Board of Directors meeting last Friday?" He rolled his eyes; her short jokes were never ending.

"It's been well actually. And yes, I was busy on Friday." He began walking towards the main part of the house, taking in the large open floor planning. "Sorry for missing the meeting. Was I on the agenda? I don't have anything to report on anyways. It's not a big deal. I don't even have that large of a stake in the company. Mom's leaving it to you at the end of the day."

She scoffed crossing her arms, "As long as you know. Someone has to keep the pieces together that nobody else cares about."

"Did I hear the door open?" Mama asked as she wiped her hands on a towel, walking out of the pantry. She was wearing jeans shorts with a green polo. No stains in sight. Her silver hair was blown out straight and hung past her shoulders, a slight curl at the ends. "Hey baby," she said as she kissed his cheek. He wrapped his arms around her and kissed her cheek back, squeezing her tighter in the hug.

"Hey Mama, do you need any help?"

"No Coraline is helping me along just fine. But you can set the table."

"Yes ma'am." As he walked towards the kitchen, he looked up at the family portrait that hung in the sitting room above the electric fireplace. It was the family portrait they took three years ago. Mama sat in a chair, with the three of us standing behind her. Everyone wore matching orange polos without a crease in sight. *Mama made sure of it by steaming our shirts in the studio.* Coraline and Casey had bone straight dark brown hair with not a lace in sight. *My fade was nice too.* Every Grant was in their proper place, perfect. Hiding the mask of the real kind of work the family business was built on.

As he went into the kitchen, grabbing the plates and forks, Coraline walked in and stirred a pot with gravy. The room was now filled with an unspoken emotion. The kitchen they stood in now was triple the size of the one they had growing up. Everything worked, the cabinets closed all the way and the plates were expensive and heavy. But they never talk about the past. Calvin remembered how excited Coraline was to play basketball growing up. It was all she talked about. She wanted to go pro after her team won the championship in middle school. She even had a good season her freshman year. But then she quit. Coraline said it was because she got bored and needed to focus on college. But Calvin knew Mama had a hand in it. Mama was always training her for excellence and basketball wasn't in that vision.

He walked past her as he left the kitchen, he turned back and looked at her. When they made eye contact, she scoffed and she began putting the food in serving bowls. Calvin accepted years ago that Coraline's mind worked much differently than his. To her, everything was family and business. Nothing else could exist. She wasn't married, she didn't have any kids. He'd be surprised if someone could even be around her tense, plan focused energy. He missed playing basketball with her as kids.

Coraline was turning 30 next year and it seemed to cover her in a tense cloud. But what did he know. He took everything to the dining room and began setting the table. Maybe he imagined setting a place for Gemini. *No too fast and too soon.* They just met. He had to prepare himself for her to never talk to him again.

As much as he looked forward to spending time with his family. He always felt different. He was the only family member that wasn't on Grant Enterprises Payroll. He genuinely just wanted to work in his library and read all the time. There was a book waiting for him in the car at this very moment. But, there was a strict rule of no distractions at the table. From cell phones to books. The front door swung open as he placed the fourth plate down. "The life of the party is here! Where's my red carpet?"

He sighed. As much as he loved his little sister, she enjoyed making an entrance while being dressed in the latest fashion, for her age group. She was wearing a burgundy ankle length body suit. "Hey Casey," he said with a head nod.

She threw her mini purse on the entry way table. "Sorry I'm late, my flight was delayed out of Houston. The grand opening went great! I even went on stage for a little bit." She stuck her tongue out and began twerking next to the dining table. "I had so much fun, those girls are super cool. I can't wait to visit again."

"Geez is that the best way to represent the Grant brand?" Coraline said walking past her, placing bowls of rice and gravy on the table.

Casey rolled her eyes, her 30-inch bundles swaying behind her. She was 25, three years younger, so she had a different drive for life than us. "Get the stick out of your ass, Coraline. I literally train the dancers and catch flights. Hey Mama!"

"Hey, sweet baby," Mama came back and hugged her, rubbing her back. "Well dinner is ready, and the table is set."

"It's just the four of us right?" Calvin asked. It wasn't unlike his uncle and cousins to make an unexpected visit to fix a plate or two.

"Yes son, it's just the four of us. Can you lead us in prayer?" Everyone grabbed hands around the table and bowed their heads.

"Lord, thank you for this food and bless the hands that

prepared them. In Jesus name we pray, amen." They all said amen. They went to wash their hands and began fixing their plates. Mama sat at the head of the table, while Coraline and Casey had the seats closets to her. Calvin never minded, being the middle child you tend to be forgotten a time or two. He usually sat next to Casey.

"So, what was so important on Friday that you missed our meeting?" Coraline asked before taking a bite of greens.

He swallowed his bite of his rice and gravy. "I was meeting someone." Everyone's eyebrows raised, Coraline's fork froze in the air. Her fist tightening around the fork.

"Meeting someone?" Casey said surprised. "I didn't know you went other places besides the library and home. Was the person she, he, they?" She was cheesing a large smile next to him.

He exhaled. "A she." He stabbed his greens. "But I don't know if I'll see her again. So, there's that."

His mother swooned, "Why do you say that honey? Did it not go as expected?" she said as she took a sip of her white wine.

"He's been in a mood; he looks sick or something. Is your heart already broken chump?" Coraline added.

He couldn't hold in his frown, "I took her out to dinner, and I thought when it was over that she wanted something more official. But I guess I was wrong."

Casey rubbed his back. "Aww man. It's okay, brother, at least you tried. Maybe she was nervous?" She said with a shrug. "Some people run from love nowadays. I mean I've broken a few hearts just this week."

Coraline scoffed. "Maybe she dodged a bullet. And you paid for dinner? How sweet? Was it with the nonexistent library money or the family's?"

His face scrunched as he stared at Coraline. She stared back with a smirk on her face.

"Who made you the family accountant? The library does generate some income, so recheck those reports 'boss lady'." He hated when Coraline got too big for her pants.

"Children, children. How many times do I have to tell you two to get along? When I'm gone, all you'll have left is each other. Please be more kind, especially at the table." Everyone sighed. Why did she have to do that, throwing around her end date like it's tomorrow.

"I didn't even start it, she did." He whispered, taking another bite of food.

"Anyways," Mama said casually. "Casey give us an update."

Casey swallowed, "Well, everything with the new location in Houston is coming along. I interviewed the perfect girls, for dancing and bottle service. I also was able to find a reasonably good DJ, under budget. I think the flyers need to be redesigned. But besides a few things, we should have a smooth soft open in a few weeks."

His mother applauded, "Excellent! You are the best. I couldn't get on a plane again after flying in from California. Good job on that launch!"

Casey beamed and lifted her shoulder towards Calvin.

"Thanks Mom I know. Anything you need." She winked at Coraline, a smile on her face. "Speaking of me being the best, I had a business proposition for you, Mama."

Calvin and Coraline groaned. "Another business?" Coraline asked. "You already tried lashes, then hair, and then nails. Now what do you want to do with Mom's money?"

Casey scoffed, "I was talking to mom." Mama looked up at Casey. "I was wondering, if I could start a Pole studio."

Mama brought her index finger to her chin, her thinking face. "A pole studio? We already have strip clubs and titty bars. What money would a pole studio bring in?"

Casey cleared her throat. "A lot actually. It could create a pipeline, see? Girls go to workshop classes, learn moves, build their confidence and bam. They could have a job if they want it. Maybe even do certifications so we can stop being taxed by a vender to do it for us. We could even host bachelorette parties, birthday parties and other events! I think it's money on the table that we can grab and make auditions easier. It has also been trending as a new way to work out and feel sexy. All the major cities have them now, even Nashville."

Mama looked out of the window, then to Coraline and Calvin, then back to Casey. "Hmm, maybe that isn't a bad idea. Do more research and present it to me on Wednesday in my office, put the time on my calendar before someone else grabs it."

"Yes," Casey squealed. As Mama, Casey, and Coraline began talking about market opportunities on the West coast, Calvin began to daydream, thinking about Gemini and the sound of her laugh. Would it be crazy that he imagined her sitting next to him at the dinner table? Whispering to each other while everyone else talked business. She hadn't responded to his text yet but he knew she saw it. It had only been a couple of hours, but he missed her.

After dinner, Calvin wiped down the table and began washing the dishes. Coraline had already left. Casey strutted into the kitchen and sat on the counter next to Calvin. "Okay big brother, tell me about this woman. I can tell your mind was drifting more than usual during 'business talk'".

He sighed while scrubbing a plate. "I've never met a woman like her. She didn't even judge me when I told her I was Bi. I really fuck with her and she's a reader. It's like she glows, but I think I fucked it up. I might be coming on too strong. But I really like her and she keeps pulling away. I can't help my feelings at this point."

Casey pouted her lips. "Well how long have you known her?"

Calvin gave Casey a sideways glance. "Well if you count today... 3 days."

Casey's jaw dropped. "Bro, you have to cool down and take your time with her. You don't know her past."

He slowly rinsed the plate. He didn't even think of her point of view. "I think she said she's been single for a minute but I can't remember."

"Yea see. It's different for women, especially black woman. We have to be in a good space to be vulnerable." Casey fake coughed. "Wait, she is black right?"

He kicked her dangling feet. "Of course, she's black, I'm all black everything."

Casey raised her hands. "Sorry I just wanted to make sure. I met a nice white man in Denver three months ago and I almost folded."

Calvin stopped doing the dishes and looked at her. "Care to elaborate on that?"

She did a loud fake laugh, kicking her feet in the air. "Anyways, back to you, I think you should work on being more patient with her. She'll come around, just show her that you're there for her you know? Be her friend first, you learn more about her that way."

He placed the dish on the drying rack. "Thank you little sis. You really helped me feel better."

She put her hand over her heart, "I'm glad to be the glue that helps keeps the family together." She jumped off the counter, "Welp I'm headed home to make a phone call. It just might be Greg."

Calvin scowled at her, "Didn't I tell you my friends were off limits?"

Casey smiled, "Don't worry, I'm not dangerous." She put on her shades as she kissed Mama goodbye.

As Calvin drove home, he thought about the advice Casey gave him. Show her that you're there for her, take your time, be a friend. He really did have to be patient. Gemini was worth any amount of time. But he couldn't wait forever for her to talk to him. That also meant that he wasn't going to text her every five minutes and leave 30 voicemails. That would be crazy behavior.

83 | *The Book at the Bar*

Chapter Eight

Gemini

I apologize for the inconvenience, but I will call you back once I do some thorough research into your case. Helping Human Helpers is always here for our people. Thank you," Gemini slammed the phone down. She knew she needed a break to think. All her mind did was race. It was Monday, the most dreaded day for a HR professional. Between the virtual orientation link not working for 2 hours (which led to a flow of calls and voicemails) and the one-off questions about paycheck copies and updating addresses, her forehead was throbbing. She'd gotten tired of helping people and it wasn't even 10am yet.

Then the Saturday flashbacks played on repeat in her head. The site of Calvin walking out of the shower, his teeth on her lips. *Oh his dark tasty lips.* The way his nails felt digging into her. When she imagined him whispering good girl in her ear, she could melt in her office chair. But the heartbreaking look in his eye when she got into that car made her feel guilty. She shouldn't have run off like that. The anxiety attack was bad but maybe he would've helped. She didn't even give him the chance to. She could've communicated with him better, even if they did just meet.

When she finally made it home Saturday morning, all she could do was cry. She called Serena last night to try to distract herself, but even Serena was confused about why she left. The only piece of advice she gave about the situation was, "Quit getting in your own way about the things you want bitch. Especially since the dick was good!"

Gemini should text Calvin back. They didn't talk at all yesterday and she genuinely wondered what he was doing. Did he go to Sunday family dinner? Did he mention her? She couldn't stop thinking about him. She wanted more of him. She didn't even know what he had for breakfast and she was curious.

She began biting the edge of her pen. Should she start taking Calvin more seriously? What if he was like everyone else and just wanted some pussy? If it was a friends with benefits situation, that's okay. Nobody said anything about dating officially. Things moved fast at first but she didn't want anything serious right now. Her work projects were growing, without her pay growing the same. It drove her insane. If her desk phone rang again, she was going to scream into it.

But they did have a romantic dinner. And her credit card never got charged for the room, she just saw the receipt in her email. He must've paid for that too, even though they agreed that she would pay for it. She had to at least say thank you. *Be a big girl and talk to him.*

Gemini: Good morning, thank you for paying for the room. You didn't have to do that

Calvin Lips: Good morning. You're welcome. I figured since you weren't staying in the room, you shouldn't have to pay for it

Of course he had to say it like that.

Gemini: I'm sorry I ghosted you like that. I should've just stayed in the room with you. I missed talking to you yesterday

Calvin Lips: I missed talking to you yesterday too

Gemini: Can you forgive me?

Calvin Lips: Of course baby. I just want to let you know that I enjoyed all of Saturday with you, not just the hotel. I wouldn't force you into anything you don't want to do. But I had to let you know how I feel. I genuinely like you

Gemini: I like you too.

That's why I'm scared.

Well, at least they felt the same about each other. That confirmation made her feel a little bit better. His sudden vulnerability made her melt more. It's rare to find someone, let alone a man, that lays things out plain. Her desk phone rang again, and it made her jump.

She needed a break from the noise pollution. When she talked to the caller through how to complete their I-9 form, her Aunt Lorraine came to her mind. She still lived in Valdosta and Gemini always loved visiting her. She always made gingerbread cookies and they would sit in the backyard together, enjoying the silence as they watched the trees and grass sway back and forth. The stillness always calmed her.

As Gemini walked out of her building, after work, the July Georgia heat began to bake her skin, she called Aunt Lorraine's house phone. She answered on the fifth ring, "Hello honey everything okay?" Just hearing her aunt's voice made her relax.

"No, not really, are you busy this weekend?"

She heard a pot clamoring in the background, "Nope. Your cousin came by the other day and cut the grass for me. I ain't going nowhere soon though. Why?"

Her eyes welled up, "Can I come over on Saturday? I've been super overwhelmed and want to spend some time with you." She tried not to break down as she got in her car.

"Oh suga," her aunt's southern twang tugged at Gemini's heart. "Of course, you can honey, want to bake cookies or have dinner?"

She chuckled wiping her eyes, "Can we do both? I can help with dinner."

"Of course! Now let me see what I have and we can throw a little something together. I'll check my freezer and defrost somethin'. How does that sound?"

"It sounds great Auntie. I'll see you in a few days."

"See you then suga." The call ended and she felt like her brain wasn't swirling as much anymore. Just the thought of sinking her teeth into a hot gingerbread cookie made her smile. She'll get to be around her family and have some desserts.

Calvin Lips: Do you want to facetime later?

Gemini: I'd love to

She smiled to herself. Even though she's been hot and cold with him, he still wants to talk to her. She hoped they would continue moving at her pace. It just seemed like a lot to open up to him.

When she came home from work, she took a much needed blazing hot shower while blasting Ari Lennox to calm her nerves. She washed her face and exfoliated so she emerged a new woman. Then, she brushed her teeth and blew a kiss to herself in the mirror. "Every day may not be a good day, but there is something good in every day." Her aunt would say that to her whenever she had a bad day.

Now it was time for decisions, what to wear on facetime? She had to be cute, not naked, but teasing. She walked into her bedroom in her towel. Constance was asleep in her bed, in a tight black ball with her paw out. She opened all her drawers and decided that a crop top with biker shorts would do the trick.

As she was moisturizing her face, she got an incoming FaceTime call from Calvin. Shit, he still doesn't confirm beforehand? Why did he always do this? She answered but didn't show her face.

"I'm not decent yet. Why don't you text beforehand?"

Calvin's smile covered her screen and her heart warmed. "I tried but my thumb slipped on calling you sorry."

She looked down and set up her phone against the mirror. Calvin smiled wider when she came in view. He was standing in his kitchen washing the dishes. Even though the moisturizer wasn't settled in her skin, she still let him see.

"What do you mean not decent? You look beautiful Gem, and your body looks amazing. Like damn."

She smiled at him. "Thank you," she went back to rubbing in the moisturizer. "How was work today?"

He shrugged scrubbing the dishes. "The most interesting thing to happen today was me kicking an old man out of the teen corner for trying to hide in there after 4:00pm." Calvin shook his head. "Besides that, I did inventory for the week, ordered paper for the printer and organized some donations we got a few days ago. They save us more money than they know."

Gemini washed her hands and carried her phone down to her kitchen. She set her phone up on the utensil stand. She took her chicken wings out of the fridge and began cleaning them.

"You clean your chicken? I can trust you whew." Calvin pretended to wipe sweat from his forehead. "Good to know you know the basics."

She laughed heartily, "There are people that don't? You have to get the feathers off. At least that's what I was taught."

He nodded drying off a plate. "Me too."

Gemini was seasoning the chicken as she looked up at her phone. She was glad to see Calvin on the screen, chopping tomatoes. He was playing jazz music so she turned the volume up on her phone so she could hear it too. It was nice to do something 'ordinary' with someone else, even if it was virtual. "The music you were playing in the hotel on Saturday was really nice. Is that a playlist you made?"

"Yes I love playlists. I love music, especially R&B. It's so smooth and warm. It's like the music is giving me a hug while also covering me in honey."

"Mmm I'd love to lick honey off you," he said with a deep voice.

She gave him a look, "I'll believe it when I see it." She chuckled lightly. "What kind of music do you like?"

He chuckled, "I'm really into jazz, as you can tell." She couldn't hold in her smile. "You can laugh but jazz is relaxing. There's nothing like being in a clean house, with a candle and the sweet sound of a saxophone."

Gemini flipped the chicken and began seasoning the other side. "I wasn't coming for you. I've enjoyed the jazz selections you've played so far. What's your favorite dessert?"

Calvin paused and looked up, "It would have to be pound cake for me. What about you?"

"Definitely gingerbread cookies. My aunt and I would make them together and it would be so good. Ginger is spicy, but also sweet to me." Gemini looked away as childhood memories flooded her brain and tastebuds. She used to grab a cookie before leaving for school everyday, even in high school.

"There you go with the sweet and spicy, very on brand for you." He lifted the corner of his lips in a charming smile.

She blushed. "Yea whatever. Also, just to let you know,

I'm going to Valdosta next Saturday to spend some time with my aunt so I'll be MIA for the day. I'm looking forward to it because I haven't seen her in a while. I'm staying to help with dinner too."

Calvin smiled. "That sounds sweet Gem, it would be a good break. It sounds like you've been missing her for a while. I love hearing you talk about her."

She put the pan into the oven and set a timer. "Yea it will be and I do miss her a lot. I almost started crying when I heard her voice today."

"That's how I feel talking to my mom sometimes. Her voice just tugs at my heart strings." Calvin moved the camera so she could see him put the dishes away in his cabinet. His back muscles flexing with each stretch. He continued, "I hate when someone gives her a hard time because I won't hesitate to fight. Especially about my Mama."

Gemini chuckled at the face he made. "Yea Auntie Lorraine is the closest thing I've ever had to a mom. My 'real mom' wasn't really in the headspace to raise me. So, her sister stepped in so I could have a good life. That was when I left Florida and moved to Georgia." She sighed, zoning out at the oven. She hated thinking about her childhood. The moving, being the ackward new kid. Things weren't as easy as they could've been if her mom could've focused on her. "That move was really tough for me because I tried to take care of my mom. But it still wasn't enough. I used to hate her and blame her for everything wrong in my life.

"I had to make new friends and move into a different house.

It's hard to make friends in a new city, let alone a new state. I missed living by the beach and the constant heat. Thankfully, I made a bestie, Serena. We looked out for each other as kids and still do. The older I get, the more I understand that everything happens for a reason. Everything isn't forgiven, but I'm not seeking revenge if that makes sense. But I struggle to find peace."

Calvin looked at her with understanding eyes. "Those are big adjustments to make at the same time, especially as a kid. Adults don't always process changes like that well either. Being raised by a single parent is never easy, it always feels like something is missing. My dad was never around so I didn't get to miss him. But it would suck around Father's Day or birthday parties at school when I'd see my friends with both of their parents. My mom travelled a lot for work, but I'm still thankful for everything she did, you know? She did the best she could with what she had. Now to see her at this point in her life, I'm proud of her. Everything takes time."

They nodded, looking at each other on the screen. Gemini was now washing dishes, while Calvin was making a salmon salad. She could get used to having Calvin around. He was sweet, and he hadn't been pushing her to hang out again, whether that was a good thing or bad thing. There was something about his voice that made her want to slow down and take a deep breath. She wanted to give him a hug right now and smell his musk. She wanted to be in his arms. She wanted to be near him.

Gemini opened her work email and couldn't hold in her eye roll. Her boss kept adding things to her to do list, when she already at deadlines to meet. She began addressing the emails in her inbox, accepting a meeting with a benefits manager about their new platform for this year. If she didn't finish responding to the other 20 emails, she would never eat breakfast in time. By the time she looked at the clock again, it was 12:15pm. *Well, it's too late for breakfast now. Lunch time.*

She stretched her hand on her desk, her lunch box wasn't there. As a matter of fact, she couldn't remember making her lunch this morning. She pretended to smash her head on her keyboard. What was she going to eat today?

Calvin Lips: How's work going?

Gemini: Horrible! I forgot my lunch 😣

Calvin Lips: What do you have a taste for?

Gemini: I could smash a couple steak tacos right now from how my stomach is touching my back

Calvin Lips: Text me the address to your job. Take lunch in 20 minutes and I'll bring it to you.

What. What? Bring her lunch? Why would he bring her lunch? She didn't even know how far he was. She texted her work address and he called her when he arrived 20 minutes later. She quickly closed her laptop and went downstairs.

As she was going down the elevator, she made sure her teal

polo and black dress pants looked nice. Her braids were in two small buns at the front and down in the back. *Did he really come to bring me lunch that fast?* She stepped out of the elevator and through the glass doors. Then she saw him.

He was wearing an orange short sleeve button down shirt with khaki pants. The whole ensemble looked amazing on his dark skin. All she could think about was how his ass felt in her gasp. When he noticed her walking towards him, a cheesy smile plastered on his face. "Hey Gemini, I got you chicken and steak tacos. I didn't know what drink you got so I got options. A bottle of water, a Sprite and an Apple soda." He held up multiple bags in his hands.

Her jaw dropped. "Wow, first off, thank you so much for this food. And second, I want the Apple soda." She looked around, the courtyard was clear. She leaned forward and kissed his cheek. "You'll eat with me, right?"

He smiled bigger, "O- of course. I didn't want to assume you wanted to eat together."

"Why not?"

He shrugged. "I just wanted to make sure that you ate. You weren't about to pass out in there."

She laughed, "Yea I can't believe I forgot my lunch today. I'm usually better with taking care of myself but I've been thrown off lately."

"What do you think threw you off?" he asked as they walked to a table in the courtyard.

She shrugged. "I don't know, life, having to think at work.

Everything. But I also met someone that has kinda thrown off my axis, in a good way."

Calvin looked at her and smiled. "Thrown it off in a good way?" They sat down and Calvin handed her the food and hand sanitizer. They slowly began to eat.

"Yea, in a good way. He is very sweet. He even went out of his way to bring me food for lunch, which I really appreciate by the way. He also happens to be fine as hell. I've only known him a week and things are paying off."

He smiled with a full mouth. "I couldn't let you sit in there hungry. I had to make sure you were good."

She blushed. She was usually super careful with sharing her actual work address, but it's nice sitting with Calvin. Tacos were romantic. The 30 minutes went by faster than she wanted them to. "Welp, it's time for me to go back upstairs. Thank you again for lunch Calvin." They hugged, and she kissed his cheek again.

"You're welcome Gemini. We'll talk later?"

"Of course, babe," she said with a grin. They waved as they walked away from each other. Gemini answered phones with a pep in her voice. After she printed some employee files, she heard her phone vibrate so she checked it. Seeing Calvin Lips on her phone, made her grin.

Calvin Lips: It was really nice having lunch with you. I'm glad you ate

Chapter Nine

Calvin

As soon as Calvin read that she didn't have lunch, he sprang into action. This was his chance to show her how he felt in a friendly way. The taco order was sent before his foot was out of the door. He couldn't have his queen go hungry. Well, she wasn't officially his queen, but he could try and hope. How much trouble could a library get into with the manager being gone for 30 minutes? Would a ghost come and throw books off the shelves? Yes, but, Sherri is a friendly ghost and wouldn't hurt anyone. Everyone knew that already.

He sped back into the parking lot, still on the high from being in Gemini's presence. He wanted to text her as soon as he made it to his car. But he waited, patience. The building wasn't on fire, whew. When he got to the counter, Greg was there, checking in books. Calvin sighed; Greg rarely visited let alone helped out. He looked good behind the desk.

Calvin patted his back. "Look who stepped up behind the desk," he whispered.

"You owe me nigga," Greg whispered back. "Why did I have

to find out you weren't here from seeing your car wasn't in the parking lot?"

"How do I owe you for you doing work at a place you partly own?" Greg shrugged and Calvin took the seat next to him. "Anyways, what's new with you?"

"Not much, my girlfriend has been in a mood because I was trappin' at the house. But that was how we met so how is she surprised?"

"Damn I'm sorry man, need a place to crash?"

"Nah, it's not that bad. I just gotta travel to deliver now. No big." Calvin nodded. "So, you not gonna tell me where you went?"

Calvin pressed his lips together. "Nowhere, just went to meet Gemini for lunch. I brought her some tacos since she forgot her food."

"Look at your sprung ass. I'm happy for you," Greg said coldly. "Well since you're back, imma head out." He hit the counter, got up and left.

"You just got here man, already?" Calvin asked with his hands up.

Greg threw up the deuces and walked out. What was his problem? Was his girl really on his mind or was it something else? As he watched Greg walk away, he pulled his phone out of his pocket and texted Gem.

Gemini Babe: It was nice having lunch with you too! We should make it a thing... if you want. I know we've turned Fridays into a thing now

Calvin: I'm cool with that. You looked beautiful by the way

Gemini Babe: You did too. That color is great on you. Where's your cardigan? You're supposed to look like a librarian not a black Clark Kent I want to fuck again

Chapter Ten

Gemini

To: Gemini.Collins@HHH.org
From: HR@HHH.org
Subject: Happy Friyay HR!

Thank you for all of your help with our clients! We've consistently connected more businesses to top quality HR service for over 40 years!

Have a great yay filled weekend! And remember, help a human today!

From.
Helping Human Helpers, Inc

The Friday emails made her cringe the most. Whoever was behind the system wide emails had to have a book filled with corny lines. They had been texting each other good morning and good night messages, random songs, and meaningful questions on a daily basis for two weeks now. She found herself thinking about Calvin all the time. His mouth against her skin and the way his skin tasted. Before she knew it, goosebumps rose on her arms as she typed on her keyboard. Thinking about him made her heart race. Her computer began ringing, another call. She plastered on her customer service smile, they can hear it through the phone. "Hello! Thank you for calling Helping Human Helpers! My name is Gemini and I'm here to help you."

"Hey! Can I have a copy of our bereavement policy? My employee had a cousin pass away and I need to see if her leave time is approved."

Gemini began typing, "I can definitely help you with that. I do offer my condolences to your employee. Our bereavement policy was recently updated so I can send you an email with the most updated copy. May I have your first and last name and employee number?"

"Sure! It's Lewis Gray, 87032."

Gemini pulled up his virtual employee file to confirm that he was a HHH employee. "Great! I have confirmed your information in our system."

"Perfect! How soon can I expect it? Will I have it before the day ends?"

Gemini's fingers flew across the keyboard. In seconds she reviewed information in the system, crafted the email and the policy was getting attached simultaneously. She created a program that saved her minutes of clicking time. Then for extra measures, she highlighted the section that answered his question and more.

"Of course! The email should be in your inbox in the next 2 to 3 minutes."

He grunted. "Really? That fast." Sent. "Wow it just came

through. You work fast Ms. Gemini."

She listened to him click and review the attachment. "You're welcome! I have also attached instructions of how to submit a flower request so that flowers can be sent to the funeral home from HHH."

"Thank you maam. I didn't even know we did that! You've been a great help and very thorough. How long have you been with HHH?"

"3 years sir and have enjoyed every minute. I'm the team supervisor."

"Great! Well I'm the office manager for the CEO and I'm very pleased with the service and knowledge you provided. Is Jane your manager?"

Gemini looked up in her cubicle towards her bosses office. "Yes she is. Jane is a great leader and has brought some innovative thinking to our team."

He laughed heartily, "Yes she is! Her and I cross paths many times. I'll be sure to bring your name up. You're a great representation of our company. Have a good day Gemini."

"You too. Thank you for calling! You may be receiving a survey on my service." The line ended. She hoped he meant it because she would love to be promoted from supervisor to manager. She's already doing a manager's job, with no direct reports. They should just promote her.

That call boosted her confidence, even if the guy lied about telling her boss about her work, she still appreciated the compliment. She glanced down at the clock, 4:15pm, might as well be quitting time.

Her phone lit up again with another text from Calvin.

Calvin Lips: I high key miss you. It's been weeks. Want to meet at the bar? It is Friday

She smiled to herself as she responded.

Gemini: Only if you bring a book too

She smiled to herself swinging side to side. Who was she now? She didn't date before meeting Calvin. A sexy bookworm was delivered to her and she took advantage. Now, she was falling for this man, hard. More flashbacks of how he sucked her lips like her clit, his lips leaving butterflies kisses on her thigh, his hands gently but forcefully grabbing her waist and pulling her into his mouth. She wanted to see him again and couldn't wait. She just saw him last week but that felt like forever now. She threw her work laptop into her bag, locked the drawers and hurried out of the door.

When she pulled into the bar, she noticed the only other car in the parking lot. Calvin's. When she walked in, she saw that he was sitting in the seat next to *hers*, at the corner of the bar. His head was down, a book open under his nose. She smiled widely. There was nothing that turned her on more than watching a man lose himself in a book. Since he didn't notice her when she walked in, she walked in a wide circle around the room so she could appear behind him. She traced her finger up his spine. He jumped and turned around. "Is anyone sitting here?" she asked. They laughed together as he stood up.

They gave each other a long hug and he kissed her cheek, resting his hands on the lower part of her back, his thumb brushing against the fabric of her shirt. She loved how he hugged her. It was like his arms perfectly cradled her back. It seemed like whenever they touched, there was an energy exchange. He shouldn't have the power he did over her body. He could tell her to get on her knees and she would right there and then in front of the empty chairs and Al.

"Hey baby girl," he said against her ear. The flood ran in between her legs. *So silky.*

She giggled as she pulled away, "Hi babe, how was work?"

He pulled her chair out and she took her seat. "It was okay. Two people are on vacation this week, so I've had to pick up some slack. But, it's nothing too serious. Our drag reading circle went on schedule. The kids enjoyed it. But I'm glad it's over so I can be close to you." He did his classic half smile that made her feel like she was sinking deeper in the puddle in her jeans.

She playfully rolled her eyes and shoved his shoulder, "Stop trying to make me seem important."

He gave her a serious look. "You are important to me Gemini. I knew from the exact moment I saw you sitting here. The way the light danced around you, how you giggled at certain parts of your book, watching your chest rise and fall during the spicy scenes. I was locked in with you. I'm still shocked at myself for approaching you. I was so nervous, but when the time came I had to take my chance. No matter what the future brings."

She looked at him in the eye. A few minutes passed as they studied each other's eyes and features. She wasn't expecting him to turn so serious. She licked her lips maintaining his eye contact. "Am I important to you because I broke your dry spell or because I swallow? It would be hard for me to walk away from some free head."

He laughed heartily, leaning over the bar. "You know that's not what I meant." He chuckled. "You're sweet, funny, beautiful and really down to Earth. You also are an avid reader, which is hard to come across nowadays. The fact that we had a whole conversation about tropes still blows my mind. I usually save the book conversations for work. Texting you throughout the day really makes me smile. You genuinely have a good open heart. I'm just grateful you gave me a chance to talk to you, that day and now."

Her stomach fluttered. It sounded, and felt like, he was catching real feelings too. She wanted him to keep chasing her. As long as Calvin was obsessed with her, she felt good. They looked at each other for a few seconds.

"So how are you feeling about me?" He asked her with longing in his deep eyes. How could she put into words that she wanted to sit on his face while also cuddle with a book with no official title or commitment yet. She wasn't ready. Her throat became really dry. She hasn't been in a committed relationship in three years. Everything in her life had been going fine, so she wasn't searching for the man of her dreams. There was no need.

Their meet cute was accidental, not intentional.

"Your usual Gemini?" Al asked, adding a much needed distraction.

She looked up at him with relief. "Yes please. Thank you".

"I figured," he placed a napkin down in front of her and placed the drink on it.

She took a big sip. Even though she might get a brain freeze from the frozen Strawberry Daiquiri. She had to deflect. When she placed the drink back down, Calvin was still looking at her waiting. "Feeling is such a strong word, right? I mean it's only been a few weeks and I'm not emotionally open to a relationship right now. I'm sorry I left you at the hotel, I should've opened my mouth. It was just a lot to process at that time." She took another sip as the disappointment grew on Calvin's face. "But I vibe with you and I enjoy talking to you every day too. I feel more comfortable with you, and I don't think you would kill me." Gemini chuckled and took another deep breath as she looked at her drink. Then she looked into his expecting listening eyes.

She continued, "But I can't hide my attraction to you. I've never done car stuff with... anyone. You make me feel good Calvin. You also look very sexy while you're reading. I've never been with someone who enjoys it as much as I do. You are a breath of fresh air to me, honestly. I really enjoying talking books and spending time with you. It also made me feel very special when you brought me lunch. I don't have many people looking out for me here."

He nodded his head looking away from her. She swore he

blushed. "Nice um, thank you and I've already forgiven you for the hotel. So you don't have to mention it again." The music filled the space between them. "Do you mind if I keep reading then? Is the lighting good for you?" Calvin said with a chuckle.

She smiled back. "Yea go ahead I'm taking my book out now. I just started it yesterday."

"Nice." They escaped into their book worlds for an hour. When she finished her drink, he bought her another. Then she bought him another drink. "Why are you buying me drinks?" he asked her.

"I mean, do you want to get drunk with me or just get me drunk?" she said with a laugh.

"Both." He said with a chuckle, lifting his glass. "What should we toast to?"

Gemini thought, "Hmm, let's toast to me sitting on your face before the night is up."

His eyebrows lifted and they tapped glasses. "Fuck yea," they kept their eyes on each other and they sipped from their glasses. "Do you want to go outside? It's getting kind of loud."

"Of course," she said with a sly smile.

They sat at their couch and continued talking. His arm wrapped around her shoulders as she nestled her head in his neck. She wished she could drink his scent, whiskey with a natural earthy undertone. As Calvin talked about the books he repaired at work, Gemini tried to get even closer to him, leaning on his every word, absorbing his voice into her skin to remember forever.

When she looked up again, it was dark outside with an almost cool breeze passing by. Calvin looked down at her, "Do you want to go to the library? I can give you an exclusive night tour."

She sat up and brushed her shoulder against his. "Oh? Is this the tour you take all the pretty girls on?"

He chuckled. "No just the woman I am interested in."

She looked at his lips. "The woman? As in just one?"

He gently brushed his thumb on her chin, looking into her eyes. "Yes, you're the woman. The only woman I'm interested in. My baby."

They stood up. Gemini tried to untie the knots in her stomach from him saying, my baby. It was so possessive, so serious. "I'll be your baby then, text me the address and I'll meet you there. After I use the bathroom and close out my tab."

Gemini watched Calvin as he turned the key to the library and turned the alarm off from his phone. She followed reluctantly at first. The dark shadows of the aisles and books made it seem, too quiet. "Are you sure it's okay for us to be here?" She whispered.

"Yes, I promise. I'm one of the owners and I have the keys". He jingled them to make his point. "We won't get in trouble or anything," he said back in a normal voice.

She couldn't help but to whisper in the library. It was customary and expected. But being here, with Calvin, made her feel like she had an after-hours backstage pass to one of her favorite places. "I'm ready for the tour," she said with a low giggle.

He suddenly stood right next to her, intertwining his fingers with hers. "It's dark, I don't want you to get lost." She rested her chin on his shoulder and kissed his cheek.

"Thank you, I am accident prone and would hate to sue you." As soon as she finished the sentence, she tripped on the rug in front of the elevator. He held her arm and grabbed her waist, keeping her steady.

"You weren't kidding," he said with a chuckle.

"It was your idea to come here after a few drinks." He pressed the elevator button and the doors swung open. His hand stayed at her hip and she didn't want him to move it as they stepped inside.

As the lift rose, he cleared his throat. "About a year ago, the city was threatening to close this library. There was a protest that turned ugly because of a banned book being available for check out. The parent found it in the kid's possession and enraged the community about it. So, a close friend and I, honorable mention to my mom, came together and bought it privately."

The elevator stopped again and he held the doors as she walked out. He resumed his spot next to her, his cologne brushing across her nose again, making her want to bite his neck.

"If yall own this library, how do you turn a profit if it's not from the books?"

"Donations, but we do rent it out as an event space sometimes. We've hosted weddings, photoshoots. You'd be surprised how many people want to have the library as a backdrop. We also host silent reading parties. That's where we collect most of our donations. Most of our books were donated from the community too."

As they walked around, she brushed her fingers against the spines of the books. "Libraries are so important. I'm glad the community still contributes, especially after that debacle. It must be a lot on you. But I'm glad everyone helped give a push too."

"Yea, I just want to make a positive impact for the readers coming behind me. Reading wasn't always available to us."

She nodded, "That's very true." Calvin hummed in her in her ear. She turned towards him, their noses lightly brushing against each other. She didn't even know what book section they were in, just that she was in the arms of her man. *Well he wasn't officially her man.* But he was with her right now. She leaned towards him and they kissed, exhaling into each other. The silence around them amplified their moans. All she could hear was her heartbeat in her ears. She couldn't wait anymore.

His hands squeezed her waist as she brought her arms to rest on his shoulders. Her fingers dancing on the back of his neck, lightly brushing his hair. She turned her head and pulled him closer, his hands reaching for her ass. "Fuck Gemini," he moaned. His hard dick rested on her pelvis. Her hand brushed his ear, down the front of his neck and chest. She began rubbing the front of his jeans and he moaned against her puckered lips.

"How does that feel darling?" she whispered in his ear. Their lips met again. But with even more power. He nibbled her bottom lip. "That good huh," she breathed. His hands squeezed and rubbed around her body in a way that made her knees shake. She wanted to rip his shirt in two. "What do you want to do to me?" she egged.

He growled and grabbed her from under her knees, lifting her. She couldn't hold in her laugh with her arms around his neck. He placed her on one of the tables. She smiled as Calvin kissed her neck, wrapping her legs around his waist. The windows brought in the dim streetlight, barely lighting their faces, emphasizing the shadows. "You are so amazing Gemini. You feel so fucking good. I think about you all the time. I want to eat you up right here."

She moaned, "Right here baby? Are you sure?" He unbuckled her jeans and pulled them off at her feet. He looked at her in the eyes as he kissed her knee, inner thigh, and the back of her thigh as he slid off her panties. He gently licked her palace, his tongue moving faster than she could follow. Her back arched to lean into his mouth more. He wrapped his arms around her knees and sucked her louder and louder. Her screams echoing off the walls. If someone was in here, they would know exactly what was going on.

She couldn't take it anymore; she felt her rise. "Oh –!" she gasped, he continued to suck as her juices came. Her eyes rolled to the back of her head, her nails lightly brushing the back of his head and neck. Her hips lurched again and he pulled her closer. Her ass hung off the desk. Gemini squeezed her eyes as her body shook against Calvin's lips. How did he know his way around her already? She tried to pull him up but he refused. "Lay back and take what you deserve," he said with a growl. She gave up her fight and gave into him. After she came for the fifth time, she couldn't breathe and all she saw were stars on the ceiling and the beautiful chocolate man rising from in between her legs with the wide, wet smile on his face.

When he stood up over her, the dim light glistened on his drenched lips. She still couldn't compute words. "You look delicious on that desk," he said licking his lips. "But we should get home." She nodded as she sat back up, groaning.

"I guess you're right," she said with an exhale. "I don't even feel like driving, but I guess I have to." He grabbed her hand and helped her down from the desk. She was surprised it even held her weight.

As they walked out of the closed, dark library hand-in-hand, Gemini's knees wobbled. *I guess I can cross that off my bucket list.* "Do you need a ride home?" he asked concerned.

"No, no I'll be fine. You just took my soul back there so I'm trying to find it again." He walked her to her car. "Thank you for tonight, we always have a good time, don't we?" She lightly pushed his chest.

He caught her hand on his chest. "Yes, we do. I had a good time too, the whole time." He kissed her hand. "Text me when you make it home, please?"

She took a step towards him and lightly kissed his lips, tasting herself. "I'll do that, good night babe."

"Good night Gem." As she got in her car and began to process. She realized just how deep her feelings were growing for Calvin. She held her hand to her chest. *Maybe this is serious.* She couldn't wait to unload to Auntie Lorraine tomorrow. Oh shit, I didn't give Serena an update.

Gemini: I made it home, sorry about the late responses

Serena My Main: Mmhm I hope the dick was worth it. I'm glad you made it home safe tho

Gemini: I made it home

Calvin Lips: Awesome! Me too. Tell Constance I said good night. Sleep tight

Chapter Eleven

Calvin

While Calvin was finishing checking in books from the box outside, a tiny pink bubble purse was placed on the counter. He looked up, it was Casey taking off her shades. "Hey brother! You look like such a nerd around all these books, with your adorable glasses." She poked his forehead. She was wearing a bright pink romper.

"Shh," he said quickly. Then he smiled at her. He wasn't used to in person family visits. Everyone usually teased him about the library at dinner, why volunteer other days. "Hey sis, what's goin on?"

"Can I take you to lunch?" She whispered. "I had some free time and wanted to check on you, per our last conversation at dinner." She wiggled her eyebrows at him.

He nodded and logged out of the station. He notified his staff that he was going to lunch and grabbed his wallet from the office. He held the door open for Casey as they walked out.

"Can we go somewhere casual?" Casey offered. "I'm not in the mood for fancy."

Calvin pulled out his phone. "Sure, we could go to the burger spot down the street."

"Great, text me the addy." Calvin sent the address as he walked to his car.

He found a decent table and placed his order by the time Casey pulled in. Even though they were Atlanta natives, Casey had a horrible sense of direction. He ordered an extra side of fries just in case her food took too long. "Would you believe I got fucking lost? Why do so many streets look the same? I hate driving. Ugh, I wish I could Uber Black everywhere" she exhaled. Thankfully, there was no line and she quickly put in her order and joined Calvin. "So give me an update on Gemini." She delicately placed her purse on the table.

He rolled his eyes. He never understood the purpose of a such a small bag. "There isn't much to tell. I brought her lunch because she forgot it, I wasn't about to let her be hungry at work. We just saw each other last night and she still hasn't left my mind. To be real, I fall deeper in love with her every time we make eye contact."

Casey pouted, "That's so fucking cute. Look at you showing her that you care. That is growth. What did she say?"

"I think she was excited. We ate lunch together and she gave me a kiss goodbye on the cheek."

Her eyebrows raised, "In public?"

He nodded, "Yea it surprised me too. She makes me really happy."

"I hope I can find someone to love me like that. But he would have to be rich and meet my list of standards of course. I don't plan on getting work done but it takes money to look this good. I mean think about my waxes, nails, facials. I'm sorry this isn't about me."

"Speaking of you, how did mom like your presentation? I think it's a good idea."

She sighed looking away. "I delayed it." Casey rested her head in her hand. "I'm honestly super stressed about it. I mean, I'm only 25. I haven't been doing this job for 8 years. But I have to somehow put this bomb ass presentation together."

He shrugged. "I've seen you do a bunch of presentations. You literally train people across the country. You basically rebuilt our training program from the ground up. You do have a brilliant, organized mind Casey."

She sighed. "That's not what I mean. I haven't presented anything to Mom one on one in a while. What if she hates it or asks a question I can't answer."

"Then write it down and say you'll get back with her. Mama can be a little intimidating when you're in her office. But she does mean well. She only asks more of you because she knows you can do it."

"Do you think I can do it?" She asked him.

Calvin was taken aback. He was thankful when Casey stepped into the family business. She'd been growing into a true professional. "Of course I do! You're better than me. At least you're contributing to the family. You're able to organize and teach. Training is teaching, and teaching is a skill. I also think you're a natural born leader, like the rest of us. Just how Mama intended."

They both laughed. "Thank you, it just gets intimidating you know? I'll always be the baby but I'm also smart. Even if my bachelor's degree is in dance."

"You literally train pole dancers Casey, you're putting your degree to work."

She punched his arm. Why did all the women in his life like beating him up? "Shut up Calvin. I was thinking about going back to school like everyone else in the family."

"You want an MBA too?"

Casey nodded.

"Hell yea, do it! You're young Casey, and the degree can be useful practice, if you ever want to do your own thing." Calvin's order came and was placed on the table in front of them, with the extra order of small fires. He handed the fries to Casey. She began to devour them.

"You're always looking out for me big brother," she said as she put a fry in her mouth.

"You're not about to be hungry in front of me." When she finished the fries, the salad she ordered came. They continued talking about Casey's travels and the life stories of the different dancers. Calvin's heart warmed talking to his sister. It was refreshing to talk to her outside of a Sunday. He needed to do this more.

When they finished their food, neither moved. "So after dinner you talked about some guy in Denver. Do you want to talk about it?"

Her face looked shocked. "You heard that? Ha ha." She looked at her Apple Watch, "You know what I have a um virtual meeting. I need to make it back to my condo to take it."

Calvin's eyebrow arched, "You're usually done with work in the afternoon. But you scheduled a meeting?"

She stood up, "Uh huh. I love you big bro." She blew him a kiss and floated to her car. Calvin knew there was more to that story. But he guessed it wasn't his business yet.

Chapter Twelve

Gemini

Gemini pulled into her aunt Lorraine's driveway. The house looked the same, besides the fresh coat of paint. The front yard grass was manicured and perfect, as always. If there was anything her aunt loved, it was her yard. Her uncle Melvin accidently drove across her yard and left tire tracks two months ago. Their sibling rivalry was never ending. The neighbors had to get involved because they were fighting in the backyard… at their big age. Aunt Lorraine just turned 50 this year and Uncle Melvin was 3 years younger than her. There were four siblings in total. The other brother and sister never returned phone calls, so they had to keep looking out for each other.

When she got out of the car, she texted Calvin.

Gemini: Made it to my Aunt's, I'll call you when I leave

Calvin Lips: Bet! Tell her I said hello and enjoy yourself. Also, bring me back these amazing cookies you keep talking about

She chuckled as she read his message, walking towards the front door. Even though new plants lined the walkway to her door, her home always seemed frozen in time. She smiled as she rang the doorbell.

When the door swung open, Aunt Lorraine stood there with open arms. "Hey honey, how are you?"

Gemini's eyes warmed. "Hey auntie." She dove into her arms, nestling her head in her neck. The smell of vanilla and ginger was fresh on her aunt's shirt. Aunt Lorraine rubbed her back and rocked her side to side as the door closed behind them, squeezing her tight. "I missed you."

"I missed you too sugar." Aunt Lorraine kissed her cheek as she pulled back. "Now I just finished the gingerbread cookies and I was fixin' to make some coffee. Want me to make you a cup?"

"Yes, please. It smells great in here already." As Gemini took her shoes off and walked inside, it was like a weight was taken off of her. She was consumed by memories in the home, from when she moved in, to her high school graduation party in the backyard and when she moved out.

The home had three bedrooms but one room had been converted into a sunroom library. The library extended to the living room with a grand black bookcase that stretched the length of the wall behind the couch.

Gemini approached the shelf and admired the collection. The books were well taken care off. "You know Gemini, one day I won't be here anymore. I want you to get the books you want before anyone else. I even added it to ma will. I'll be damned if

Melvin gets to em first. I ain't scared to fight his punk ass."

"Auntie!"

Aunt Lorraine scrunched her face as she poured the coffee in the cups, arranging the cookies perfect on the plate. "I ain't scared. I'll say it to his face too. Nah where do you want to sit?"

Gemini held the outside door open, "Let's sit outside." Auntie smiled as she carried the serving tray.

They sat down under a large umbrella outside. A book in both of their hands. Aunt Lorraine was rereading *Becoming by Michelle Obama* and Gemini brought her new current read *Act your age, Eve Brown by Talia Hibbert*. When Gemini finished her chapter, she looked at her aunt to find her already looking at her. "You've met someone."

Gemini coughed and patted her throat. "What? Met someone? I mean- uh." She grabbed the cup of coffee and swallowed as her aunt gave her, *the look*. "Yea I met someone. We have hung out a few times and he brought me lunch last Wednesday. We hang out at the bar and read together. I wasn't expecting it and it was weird. Every time I'm around him I just relax. I've never felt that before. Even with what's his name I had to think for him. Calvin thinks for himself. I mean he planned our first date to the tee and I deserted him after because I got scared."

Aunt Lorraine gave her the look again. "You deserted him honey?"

She twirled her thumbs, "We hung out late and I left early when I didn't really have to. But he hasn't held it against me or anything. It just makes me feel more guilty, like I don't deserve someone as nice as him. I didn't expect him to want to keep talking to me. But yet, here we are."

Her Aunt hummed and sighed, a rare Georgia breeze blowing in her grey shoulder length silk press. Her chestnut skin shining in the shade of an umbrella. Even though she was aging, it was happening with grace and wisdom. Her rich orange nails tapped on the table as she observed Gemini. "It sounds like he cares about you dear."

"Okay so? I care for Constance. I would care for a pair of shoes or something. But how do I know if he really cares for me and not for what I do? This whole thing could be pointless."

"Well, the best way to know how a man feels about you, is tuh read his actions. A true man, is a man of action. If he wants something, he will go for it. And it sounds like this man is very interested in you. You're even glowing a little bit." She laughed. "Even I can sense it sweetheart. You have been staring at that phone, like you're waiting fa something. You're waiting for that man to text you."

Gemini chuckled to herself, "Yea. I told him I would be here. But even still. He has been very sweet towards me and he has been showing me with his actions. But I'm worried about consistency. I don't want him to dump me in two weeks because I'm not *fun* anymore."

"That's how everyone feels honey. But if he is mature, he'll be there fa ya in the fun times and low times. Even though I've neva married, that doesn't mean I aint had relationships with folk."

"Ugh auntie don't say it like that."

Her aunt took a sip of coffee, "What? I know about people. I lived a life you know. I went to *Freaknik* and had a blast. I destroyed my camcorder but if I could fix it-."

Gemini's jaw dropped, "Please no, I'll start to cover my ears."

Aunt Lorraine laughed at her. "Anyways honey, all I'm sayin' is, you never know what ya don't try. It seems like this young man is worth a try." She took a bite of a cookie and took another sip. "Has he mentioned anything about a future with you?"

"Not in so many words, but I'm also not rushing him. He has made his feelings known though."

Auntie nodded. "It's okay to open your heart up. It may be easier to close up and do it your own way. But, this could be somethin. I see it and I aint neva wrong."

Gemini smiled at her, then stared at the backyard. There was something about sitting in the shade outside, listening to nature and the trees move, that made her grateful. Not only was she grateful for her life, but the life of her aunt. She didn't know how often her cousins came by to see her, but damnit she was going to start making more of a point doing it. Family is important.

All of the points Auntie made were valid. She had to at least try something with Calvin and open her heart up. "Auntie can you wrap up some cookies for him? His name is Calvin. I've talked up your gingerbread cookies too much."

Auntie chuckled, "Mmhm. You neva share my cookies with just anyone. I still send some to Serena every now and then."

Chapter Thirteen

Calvin

Calvin grabbed the recently checked in books and put them on the cart. There was something calming about doing the router and seeing what people returned. Even though his headphones usually had *John Coltrane* playing, he decided to put on *If I was Your Man by Joe*. Gemini continued to dance around his mind so much that he thought he saw her around every corner. He imagined singing in the rain to her in a black leather suit. Even though they had only known each other 3 weeks or so now, he wanted to be her man officially. But he would be patient.

Just as he was placing *You Made a Fool of Death With Your Beauty* on the shelf, Greg suddenly jumped in front of the cart. "Ha!" Calvin jumped and accidently pushed the cart. The wheel hit Greg's toe making him yelp.

"Shh this is the library nigga," Calvin whispered.

Greg rolled his eyes. "I own this library too." He whispered. "Can we talk in your office then? *Nigga*," rubbing his big toe with a frown.

Calvin pushed the cart back behind the front desk and went into his office. His office was only big enough to fit his desk and two chairs in front of it. *I should've brought Gemini in here and bent her over the chair.*

Greg cleared his throat as Calvin sat down. "So I wanted to talk to you about something."

"Sure, what's going on?"

Greg rubbed the back of his neck and looked away from him. "I was reviewing the camera footage from Friday night."

Calvin's eyes went wide. "Camera footage? From inside the library Friday night?" He had Gemini on a desk with her legs in the air that night…

Greg gave him a sideways glance. "Uh huh. I don't mean to be in your business or nothing. I deleted the… parts before anyone else could see, or hear." He looked away from him. Was that jealously in his eyes?

Calvin covered his face. "Shit that's embarrassing. I completely forgot about that."

"You did your thing man, had her shaking and shit. I was like damn he's eating her up. I wish I got some head like that."

Calvin looked at Greg up and down. Greg maintained his eye contact with him. Was he shooting his shot? Or was Calvin reading the room wrong? They've been friends for over 10 years. He remembered high school Greg that was on the varsity football team fingering girls in his car after the games. He had to be careful with how he responded, but also get information. "I mean shit do you want some."

Greg made eye contact and rubbed his beard, licking his lips as he eyed Calvin. "I do." Then the room was silent, filled with unspoken tension. Calvin looked away and started rubbing his palms on his jeans. Was the room getting hot? Or was it just him? "Let me get a move on, I'll hit you up later." He nodded at Calvin and left the room feeling like a sauna mixed with confusion. *What did that mean?*

Calvin fixed his tie as he went up the elevator. The quarterly board meeting was mandatory for all stakeholders. His mother made sure to remind him yesterday. It's been another full week since he's seen Gemini. Even though they've texted, she hadn't mentioned anything about hanging out again. He didn't blame her. He was still thinking about the "study taste session" in his library. He had to be more forward with her. He was not about to lose her. He just couldn't. A man knew when he was in the presence of an amazing woman and Gemini was her.

When he walked in, he nodded to Coraline, his VP big sister and kissed his mother on the cheek. The table was large black oval shape to fit all five stakeholders. His mother, Darlene Grant, Coraline, himself, Casey, Lenny, their accountant, and Steven their marketing manager. The other leaders in different regions joined the meeting virtually. Casey walked in wearing a bright pink skirt suit, her matching *Telfar* purse in tow. She pulled her laptop out of her bag and began preparing to take minutes.

Mama found that Casey acting as secretary during meetings was the best way to maintain her attention. All it did was keep her from taking her phone out during the meeting.

Mama took out her notes and stood up. "Before we start the agenda, I have an announcement to make." His stomach dropped to his knees. *This wasn't good.* In all of the board meetings he's sat in through the years, she's never gone off the agenda. "I'm announcing my retirement. My eldest daughter, Coraline will happily step into the role of CEO. We will transition the role in officially the last week of August, for paperwork purposes. But I have removed the last of my belongings from my office, so my baby can move right in." She danced excitedly as the people on the screen cheered.

"Congrats Darlene! You've done it!"

"Now you can buy that beach house and relax Ms. Grant. Congratulations! You'll be missed."

Mama beamed, "I'm so glad my children have helped this business continue to grow." Calvin looked at Coraline. She was as pale as a ghost. *That wasn't good either.* She looked just as surprised as him.

Lenny raised his hand, Ms. Grant acknowledged him. "I just want to say these decades with you have been amazing Darlene. Congratulations," he raised his coffee up to her and took a sip. Calvin's mind was still wrapping around the thought of his mother no longer working with them. Who would stop their arguments mid meeting? Who is going to manage... *everything?* His brain spun the rest of the meeting. Coraline shared the same look, *shook*. Meanwhile, Casey was popping her gum typing away, seemingly unbothered from the earth shattering realization.

At the end of the meeting, Casey emailed the meeting minutes and blew kisses as she walked out of the door. Her long straight black hair swinging behind her as her heals clicked away. Everyone left the boardroom except for Calvin and Coraline. She was still glued to her chair, her eyes unfocussed. "Wow," Calvin said to break the energy in the room.

"Did that happen?" She said cold and dry.

"Yea, yea it did. I was not expecting that. I thought she would bring it up at dinner first, not here. I mean shit."

Coraline looked at him with pain in her eyes. "What are you complaining about? You barely even come here, let alone work here. I'm gonna have to do everything now. I mean, I'm already doing everything but shit. That's how it always has been." She slammed her face in her hand. "Fuck."

Calvin looked at her. Her words were a slap to the face, but she wasn't wrong. He never stepped into leadership at Grant Enterprises. The most he did was intern when he was in undergrad and that was only for a summer. It hurt him to see so much weight on Coraline's shoulders.

He walked out of the boardroom, straight to his car. He had to wrap his mind around everything. Did he have the space to help them? The library had to be managed by someone and he could only afford hire so many people. Everything seemed to be pilling on him at the same time, his heart was beating out of his chest. *Oh no.* He got in the driver's seat and grabbed his chest closing his eyes. Everything seemed to be spinning around him.

His hands became clammy as his heart began to race. Then, his phone rang, Gemini, he answered with a raspy voice. "Hello?"

"Hey Calvin. Are you okay? You don't sound good."

His tongue felt like it was swelling in his mouth. He couldn't talk. All he could do was moan and swallow to keep from throwing up.

"Calvin you're scaring me, where are you?" His hands shook as he typed in the address and his parking spot number. "Okay I got the text. I'm 15 minutes away. Are you going to be okay until I get there?" He slowly typed in yes, his hands began to sweat even more. His chest pain growing. Fuck. "I'm on the way. I'm not getting off the phone with you. I want you to take a deep breathe okay baby. Inhale 1 2 3," he inhaled. "Now exhale 1 2 3 4 5. Focus on the sound of my voice and breathing. Breath with me again honey." Calvin's lungs still stung, but he could breathe now. The sound of her voice was genuinely helping him.

Then her car came into view. She sped and parked in the space next to him. He still couldn't move out of the driver's seat. She quickly got out of her car and got into his car, settling in the passenger seat. She put her hand on his jaw, then put the back of her hand on his forehead. "Hey Calvin, can you talk yet?"

She was here. She actually came. "Ye- yes." He stammered, rasping for air. "I- I'm sorry I had a board meeting a-and it didn't go as expected. It was a-a lot. I- I'm a fuck up a- and I don't do enough a-and my sister hates me for it. N-now I d-don't know how t-to help a-anymore."

She rubbed his shoulder and began undoing his tie. "Shocking news can be a lot to process in the moment. You don't have to tell me in detail yet, but I think you should talk to someone about it. Maybe one of your sisters? If it was shocking for you, it was probably a lot for them too." She was right. She was so right. He began focusing on his breathing. *Inhale, exhale.* Coraline definitely looked overwhelmed. He had to come back and check on her.

"You are right Gem. Th- thank you for coming to check on me. I-I'll be okay." He sighed. "I h- hate that you're seeing me like this."

She pulled him into a hug. "You've been there for me, so I'll be there for you. I care about you too you know." He rested his head in her neck. He took another deep breath, breathing in her sweet-smelling perfume. The pain in his chest started to fade. There's no way she knew the hold she had on him already. Tears began falling from his eyes as she rubbed his back.

"That means a lot to me. It really does." He lifted and kissed her cheek as they pulled away. Her face lifted into a sweet smile. "I was wondering, since you're here, do you want to come over to my place tonight instead of going out? It is Friday and you haven't mentioned anything about hanging out in a minute. I've gen-genuinely missed you."

She wiped the tear from under his eye with her thumb. "I'd love that. We can definitely do that."

Chapter Fourteen

Gemini

Gemini parked her car right in front of what her GPS said was Calvin's door. She hoped that her light wash ripped jeans and pink crop top wasn't underdressed. It was a townhouse. How charming! This was the first time he ever invited her to his place. She grabbed her keys and wallet and locked her car as she walked up to his door. She knocked on the brown door.

He swung open the door with a smug smile, leaning on his forearm in the door frame. He bit his bottom lip looking at her up and down. "How do you do that?" he asked her.

"Do what?" putting her hand on her hip.

"Get more stunning every time I see you." She blushed swinging her braids around.

"Must be the melanin." He pulled her in for a quick kiss and welcomed her in. The first thing to hit her nose was the smell of vanilla partnered with a savory scent that made her mouth water. The sweet smell carried her through the townhouse. The floor plan was open so she could see everything from the living room to the kitchen. There was a small dining room table in the far corner. She recognized the kitchen from their Facetime sessions.

She was amazed at how clean everything was. There was a navy-blue rug on the dark hardwood floors. His black couch was up against the wall in front of his wall hung TV. An electric fireplace burned blue flames that reflected off the walls.

There were small and large pieces of black art hanging from the walls. The colors in the paintings, perfectly matched the décor of the home. Some were single subject of a black woman reading or a group of people dancing. Everything felt connected. If her heart was talking, she wished she brought a bag with her, more than an overnight bag. It's officially been a month of talking now. Lesbians have moved in with less time. So why couldn't they?

"Wow it's beautiful in here, I love the art and it smells amazing. How many bedrooms and baths?" She said looking at the faceless painting of a black couple dancing on a street corner. The subjects clothes moving with the music under a street lamp.

"Thank you, I did them myself and three bedrooms with two and a half baths."

"Did you have any posing subjects or just off the dome?" She asked studying the artwork.

He approached the painting she was looking at. "I mainly get inspired from my dreams; they are my muses." He looked at her and smiled as she continued looking at the paintings. He drifted into the kitchen. "Dinner is finished, I just have a lemon loaf in the oven for dessert."

Gemini began walking towards the kitchen.

"No peeking," Calvin called like he had eyes at the back of his head. His head was in the oven. "I'm getting ready to fix your plate. The bathroom is that door in the corner so you can wash your hands."

She turned and went into the bathroom. The walls were warm grey and decorated with different light blue and grey towels on floating black shelfs. She didn't know a man could decorate like this. *Or a woman lived here.* When she finished washing her hands, she sat at the square dinner table. There were two golden place mats with silverware wrapped in a napkin. Suddenly, smooth jazz music started playing on a speaker she didn't see. She looked up.

Calvin placed her plate in front of her. "Tonight we are serving medium well steak with creamy mashed potatoes and grilled asparagus."

She gasped. He plated everything beautifully and even precut her steak. A piece of cilantro sat on top of the dish. "Calvin, I have never had anything like this done for me before. This is beautiful, thank you." She pulled the collar of his shirt and kissed him. His lips surprised but welcomed their union. "This is perfect," she said as he pulled back.

"Anything for you." He made his plate and sat down across from her. The jazz music danced around them and walls as they enjoyed the meal.

After they finished eating, he picked up their plates. "I almost forgot." Gemini reached into her purse and pulled out Calvin's gingerbread cookies. "You can't say I've never done anything for you." She chuckled as she put the container on the table.

Calvin smelled the container with a smile, "Mm I hoped you didn't forget and I was scared to ask. You've talked aunties cookies up for weeks."

She watched him walk back to the sink, trying to not daydream about what she wanted to do to him tonight. As he turned the water on, she stood up. "I can help clean up and wash the dishes."

He smiled. "Aren't you sweet? Come here." She walked towards him maintaining eye contact. He stepped back as she slid in front of him. She turned off the water and poured the soap in the sink.

He stood right behind her, his hands dancing along her waist, sides, and thighs. His thumbs gently grazing the soft skin under her shirt. She couldn't hold in her moan when he kissed her shoulder. His hand spread across her stomach, pulling her into him more. She put the dishes in the water, but her hands weren't the only thing wet.

He squeezed her thighs as she exhaled and rested her weight on him. His hands working their way up her body. "Baby I can't focus on these dishes with you touching me like this."

He kissed the back of her neck. "Then don't focus on anything," he whispered in her ear.

She slowly dried her hands and turned around to face him. Her warm hands rested on the back of his neck, her thumbs brushing his jaw and the edge of his prickly chin. He looked deep into her eyes, their breaths warm on each other's lips. She turned her head and pulled him into a kiss. They fit together like a lock and key. Their chests flush against each other as Gemini kept trying to pull him closer. She could never kiss him enough times.

She lost track of the time from how he held her. She could just enjoy herself and not worry about anything outside that door. When she was with Calvin, he made her forget anything else existed. The nagging customers, projects, responsibilities. She enjoyed being in his world. He shone a light on her that she wanted to keep basking in.

He pulled away from her and she instantly frowned. *How dare he move without her permission?* But then he looked at her, with the same piercing look he gave her the night they met. The look that put her under his spotlight. "Will you be my girlfriend?" he asked. "I know we've only known each other a month or so. But I haven't stopped thinking about you since we met. I really care about you Gem and I want you to be my girl, officially."

The corner of her mouth lifted into a smile. "I would love to be your girlfriend, Calvin," she took a deep breath. "At first it scared me how comfortable I got with you. It's been so long since I was with someone who genuinely looked out for me. When you brought me lunch that day, you literally saved my life." They chuckled in each other's arms. "I'm learning that it's okay for me to be comfortable with you. I care about you and want to be with you too." The world around them stopped. She pulled his face into hers and kissed him.

Her hands crept down his muscular back, down his sides.

Feeling Calvin's breath on her neck made her relax even more. Her thumbs grazed the top of his pants, slowly coming forward, undoing his button, lowering his zipper, his breath hitched. Their lips never separated. She began tugging his pants, he pulled his briefs down. She smiled as she noticed how hard he was in her hand.

She pulled her braids back into a ponytail, glancing between Calvin and his dick as she wrapped the tie. He licked his lips observing her as she got down on her knees.

"Fuck Gemini," he whispered as she licked his head, down his length. She slowly fit all of him in her mouth and throat, her hands squeezed his waist, pulling him into her more. His breath caught when her nails brushed up and down his thigh.

He started massaging her jaw, her mouth filled with him. She looked up at him, as his head tossed back. Her index fingers played on his sensitive gap. He lunged his hips forward as she sucked even louder. "Grab my hair," she moaned.

He grabbed her ponytail and squeezed, sending a shudder through her spine. Her head dove until he was touching the back of her throat again. Her tongue wrapped around him. She couldn't even feel her knees anymore. "Look at me baby." She looked up at him, not stopping. "You are so beautiful. I love watching you and those pretty lips." He began stroking her face faster, brushing his finger down her cheek. Gemini knew he was getting close. He was going to finish before her tonight. "I'm about to come," he moaned. She smacked and squeezed his ass as he loudly groaned above her. The warmness eased into her throat, she gave one last slurp to finish. He was frozen in place his fingers gripping the cold countertop behind him. He took some deep breaths as she stood back up. "Get your ass up those stairs," he growled.

She opened her mouth and licked her lips. "Make me." His eyes went black, her grin grew. He grabbed her hips and lifted her onto the counter. He undid her jeans so fast, she barely gasped as the zipper went down. She laid her head back on the countertop as he slid her jeans from under her. When he took her panties off, the air barely hit her thighs before he dove into her. He licked his way around her creamy lips like he was following a treasure map to her pleasure points. She couldn't help but to finish on his face, listening to him slurp. She forgot they were still in the kitchen, he pulled her up so she was sitting upright on the counter.

He picked her up again and carried her up the stairs. She giggled the whole way into his bedroom. She loved when he picked her up like she was weightless. He gently placed her at the corner of his bed and turned blue lights on that made the room look like it was floating. He pulled out his phone and began playing *Calling on You by Jon B* on an unseen speaker in the room. He came back and continued kissing her like he wanted to drown. She opened up for him like a river, wanting him to swim in her for days. Gemini's arms rested around his neck, kissing him back like her lips weren't doing enough. Her hand cradled the back of his neck, her thumb brushing the back of his head. A growl rose from her chest, her body vibrated.

"Get down on your knees and put your hands behind your back." He got down on his knees at the side of the bed, crossing his wrists behind his back. Her legs spread in front of his face.

She nodded her head at him, biting her index finger. "I only want you to do what I tell you."

"Yes Gemini."

She growled, "Did I ask you to speak?"

He looked up at her. She stood up, holding the crown of his head. She bent down and kissed him again, sticking her tongue deep in his mouth as they moaned. Her fingers danced from the tip of his shoulders, across his chest, her hand right above his heart. He continued to moan at her touch as she squeezed his nipples. But she needed more, of him.

She laid back down on the bed and put her legs on Calvin's shoulders. He still hadn't moved from the position on his knees. *So obedient I love it.* His breath was warm on her entrance. "Lick me." He licked her palace long and slow as her back quivered. "Eat me out baby," he began sucking her clit in ways that made her thighs shake in response. She gripped his shoulder as he continued. He kept going until she screamed under him, which made him go even faster. He ate her like she was the sweetest fruit. The room began to spin as his tongue twisted inside and around her. Her sweet scent grew as the linen under her became soaked. She pushed his head back, his pearly teeth gleamed.

He smiled a devilish grin at her. "Now it's my turn," he stood up and left the room. She looked at the empty doorway confused. *Why did he need to leave the room?* She heard his footsteps go down the stairs, open the fridge and close it, then back up the stairs. When he returned, he had a plate of strawberries and grapes.

She brushed her hands on her thighs looking at him. "What

are you going to do with those?"

He eyed her legs, her chest and met her eyes. "Can I eat these off of you?"

She exhaled, brushing her fingers against her neck. "Yes, but I've never done that before."

He chuckled a low vibration that made her thighs quiver. "Don't worry bae." He placed the plate on the bed and grabbed a strawberry. He kept his eyes on her as her mouth slowly opened. He brought the fruit to her lips and she took a bite. The cool juice dripped from her lips, down her chin, down her neck. "Allow me," he whispered. He licked her neck and sucked on her jaw as she moaned. He picked up another strawberry and took a bite. Then he brushed it across her cheek, the red juice bleeding onto her skin. She sighed as the cool juice fell. He once again licked it. His hot tongue slick on her cool skin.

"Do you like that sweetheart?" he whispered.

"Yes bae I love it." He brushed the strawberry against her shoulder, down to her nipple.

"Good." He sucked his way down. She hoped he left hickies. *She was his now.* Her breath grew faster and faster as he sucked her nipple, gently brushing his teeth against her.

"Bite me please," he bit her nipple and she squealed, her teeth biting down on her lower lip.

Her nails brushed the back of his neck, lifting herself into his mouth more. He lifted his head and kissed her. "Lay down beautiful," her legs felt like melted chocolate as she laid back. She loved how he spoke to her. He climbed on top, never breaking eye contact. Her heart began to beat faster, his hard dick gently brushing her thigh, resting outside of her lips. "Are you ready for me?"

"I'm more than ready," she whispered in his ear. Her breath caught as he easily slipped inside of her, their moans in unison. "Yes baby," she said in-between breaths. His strokes were slow but purposeful. The way his hips worked made her grab him tighter, slickly squeezing his ass. Her hands traced the line of his muscles on his arms as he kept taking her breath away. His shoulders tightened more as he fisted the bed. He hit her sweet spot as she bit his neck, sinking her teeth inside his sweaty skin. "Right there!" She cried as she looked into his eyes, keeping his same pace. Their foreheads rested on each other as her nails dug into his back and he groaned against her lips.

"Fuck Gem you feel so good. You're so stunning baby." She came again. Just his silky smooth voice made her body shake. He bent down and whispered next to her ear "You're such a good girl Gemini. You take my dick so good." She licked his ear, he didn't miss a beat. "You look so fucking good taking all of me baby. I'm so proud of you." The way he was pouring into her, made her want to explode. She'd never had such an intimate moment like this before, with anyone. Goosebumps raised all over her body.

Her hand reached behind him and began massaging his ass. He groaned louder on top of her, tossing his head back. His eyes squeezed tighter as his mouth opened. She couldn't help but to be amazed by him. There was nothing that aroused her more than watching a man be pleasured. He bent down and began sucking her nipple again, picking up speed with his stroke. "I don't want to stop Gemini," he said with a groan.

She grabbed his neck, pulling him into her face. "Did I say stop?"

He chuckled, "No you didn't". He slowed down his pace, staring her in the eyes. Their breaths were in sync. Then he quickly pulled out, bent down and kissed her belly button, down her pelvis. He caught her by surprise by licking her clit. He kissed his way around her palace like he was a regular guest. The sound of him sucking up her juices made the bottom of her feet tingle. He came back up and kissed her. She licked his lips and kissed him deeper. He bent down and wrapped his fingers in her braids. His other hand rested on her face. His thumb gently brushing against her cheek.

Everything stopped.

They stopped moving and looked into each other's eyes like they opened a portal to something new. Their dreams were opened, the blue light wrapped around their endless connected bodies. She didn't know where her body started and where Calvin's ended. They were connected now. This was something different, the start of something new.

"Let me get on top," she whispered against his lips. He rolled onto his back and pulled her with him. She firmly planted her hands on his chest as she lowered onto him, using her hips to guide him into her. He squeezed his eyes shut as he worked his hands up her torso. Her hands feeling the stern lines on his chest.

"You look so sexy riding me, fuck Gem." He grabbed her breast, gently massaging them as he put her nipples in his mouth. It sent an instant pleasure shock throughout her body. She rolled and squeezed her hips, lightly bouncing on top of him.

Suddenly, Calvin pushed Gemini onto her back, with her legs on his shoulder. She grabbed the foot of the bed as he entered her, gasping as he rolled against her. He smacked her ass and kissed the inside of her knees. Her eyes rolled to the back of her head. They continued to flip around the bed.

When she came from riding in reverse, her body completely gave out. Her legs could only twitch as she slowly turned around and crawled to the head of the bed. Luckily she wasn't far from the pillows. As she laid her head down, Calvin lifted her leg and carefully placed a folded clean towel. Then, placed a bonnet on her head, gently tucking in her braids for her. She snuggled deeper into the pillow. There was no way she was moving now. He got back into the bed and opened his arms. She turned around and snuggled closer to him, resting her head on his warm chest, inhaling his scent. That was how she wanted to sleep every night. "Good night," he whispered in her ear.

Her eyes slowly began to close as his fingertips brushed on her back. "Good night baby." A smile grew on her face. *If that is what love making is, I'm here for it.*

She woke up to her own scream and sat up. Where was she? What happened? Her hands were shaking as she touched the cold sweat on her face. A hand began rubbing her back. "What happened baby? Are you okay?" Calvin's groggy voice said in the dark room.

She began to whimper, "Fuck this is so embarrassing. I'm sorry for waking you. I had a nightmare." Her arms were shaking uncontrollably, her shoulders shivering.

He began to stir as he sat up. He put his arm around her waist. "It's okay. Take a deep breath with me, in through your nose… out through your mouth…" They breathed together, tears falling from her face. She hated when these began to happen. She's had night terrors since she was a kid. Her ex would find them annoying and would pretend to be asleep. But Calvin was actually comforting her. "Just focus on my voice Gemini and close your eyes, everything is okay you're here with me. I got you. I won't let anything happen to you. Take another deep breath baby." She took a real deep breath, when she exhaled she put all of her weight on him. He caught her as they fell back onto the pillows, holding her in his arms as he rocked her. Her sniffles became quieter, the tears falling cold on his chest.

"Thank you," she whispered against his skin.

"You don't have to thank me, I care about you. So, I'm gonna hold you and be there for you." She exhaled deeper. It felt like he was drawing moons and stars on her back. She felt a light kiss on her forehead as she drifted back to sleep.

The first realization to hit Gemini was that the sheets she was laying on weren't her own. Then she was reminded of how Calvin held her after her nightmare. *How is he such a sweetheart?* As she stretched under the cool comforter, her hips felt tighter than usual. He did some much needed rearranging and she loved it. The flashbacks hit her like ocean waves. The dinner, kitchen island, the strawberries, the soul exchange. She felt like Bella after her honeymoon, ecstatic and relaxed. She patted the other side of the bed and found it empty. Where did he go? He wouldn't leave her in his house would he? *Yikes, pay back bitch.*

She sat up in the bed and found a t-shirt and basketball shorts folded at the foot of the bed. A handwritten note rested on top.

Come downstairs when you're ready

-Cal

She smiled and stretched then put on the t shirt. Fuck those shorts. As she came down the stairs, she smelled and heard breakfast cooking. The music was just loud enough for her to hear it, *Summer Renaissance by Beyonce* was playing. She began bobbing her head to the music, swaying her hips. When she turned the corner, she saw Calvin, shirtless in front of the stove. He was definitely dancing. He was rocking his hips, with the spatula in his hand, humming along with the music. "Good morning," she said rubbing her eyes just as he was about to do a spin.

His grin covered his face, "Good morning sweetheart. I didn't know when you would wake up, so I started making breakfast."

The cold hard wood floors woke her up more as she walked over to the kitchen and yawned. He puckered his lips and she cringed, "I haven't even brushed my teeth." She said covering her mouth.

He grabbed her waist and pulled her in. "I don't care come here." They lightly kissed. She could still taste herself on his lips.

"Mmm, what's for breakfast?" She asked peaking at the stove.

"Hashbrowns, eggs and bacon. Is that good with you?"

She kissed his cheek, "That's perfect." She began dancing next to him, swinging her arms in the air. They began singing along to the music.

"How do you like your eggs babe?" He asked dancing with an egg in his hand.

"Scrambled hard," she said bumping her hip with his.

After they ate, he began washing the dishes while she sat on the couch reading. "Hey Gem, I'm surprised I haven't asked this yet. But do you smoke?"

She chuckled, "Like cigarettes? No."

Calvin's face scrunched up. "No, like tree, the devil lettuce, Mary Jane, scooby snacks."

She laughed harder. "I do, well did. I haven't smoked in a while since my plug hit me with 'I'm out of the game to focus on my kids'. So, I haven't smoked since then. He didn't even give me a reference. I don't like pulling up to random plugs because you never know their intentions. I don't suck dick for weed."

He chuckled scrubbing the pot. "I can make a phone call for you and give you his number, if you wanted it. He's my friend Greg. He's cool. He's part owner of the library and has a girlfriend so he wouldn't push up on you or nothing."

She grabbed her 'I'd rather be reading' bookmark and stuck it into her book, "Are you serious? I would love that. I can do 100 so I can be good for a minute."

He dried off his hands and grabbed his phone. "Alright I got you, I'll let him know. Do you mind if I roll?"

She placed her book down on the coffee table. "No I don't mind at all and thanks for his info." Her phone pinged with Greg's contact information.

Calvin jogged across the living room and hopped up the stairs, returning with a black bag. He sat at the dining table as he rolled the blunt.

After they smoked, Gemini laid her head on him. His arm wrapped around her waist as they sat on his couch. They breathed together, a familiar moment between them. His playlist played, *Come Back To Me by Janet Jackson* in the background. Her body and mind felt like they were floating along with the music. She never wanted this feeling to end. The fuzzy blue blanket that was draped over them just made her want to stay there forever. She snuggled closer to him, digging her nose in his bare chest, absorbing every line, every hair. How did he always smell so good? "Calvin?"

He grunted, coming back to life. "Yea babe?"

Her stomach growled. "Do you have any snacks?"

"I do actually, let me bring them over." She whined as he stood up and walked towards the kitchen. *Nooo why did he move!?* She peaked and watched him grab a gold handled white serving tray. *So formal.* She grabbed her phone and texted

Serena.

Gemini: Bitch! I have to catch you up. Calvin officially asked me to be his gworl! I'm at his house and my guts have been rearranged in the most beautiful way ANND he was cooking breakfast when I woke up this morning

Serena: Yass bitch. You've got the morning sunrise with a song pussy

Gemini: He's got so many green flags I'm worried lol

Serena: Let your guard down sis. Not everyone has an agenda and he sounds genuinely sweet. Now stop texting me and cuddle with your man

She rolled her eyes and put her phone down, just as he placed the tray on the coffee table. One side had a variety of chips, with few hot fries. "Wow thanks for getting hot fries!" *Look at him thinking of me while grocery shopping.*

"You're welcome," he said kissing her cheek sitting back down. There was also a bowl of chili, dipping chips and cheese?

She pointed down. "There's cheese in this bowl and I thought you couldn't eat cheese."

He scooped a dipping chip in the cheese sauce. "It's vegan cheese. It's not as good, but it's as close as I can get without dying." She watched him take the bite and shrug.

She grabbed a chip and dipped it in the fake cheese. When it met her mouth, the flavoring wasn't bad. It just tasted...

different, like it was fake. But she would eat this fake cheese for the rest of her life if that meant always being this close to Calvin.

He turned the TV on, "Anything you want to watch?"

"How about a good DIY show? Watching people fix houses and backyards make me feel good. It's something about the before and after photos." He nodded while chewing. He selected *Backyard Builds*. Not a bad choice at all.

As she took note of the herringbone bone pattern they were installing, a thought occurred to her. She didn't have clean clothes and she was still in Calvin's T-shirt. "I need clothes, I didn't bring any. I don't know why I wasn't sure if I was spending the night or not."

His chest bubbling chuckle came again. "Alright I'll take you to *Target*. You can get what you want and need, on me."

She sat up and looked at him in his eye. "I'm sorry you do realize that you," pointing at his chest, "Said that to me," waving her hand around her face, "Right?"

He cringed, "Am I going to regret saying it?" She laughed menacingly, rubbing her hands together. "I won't take it back. You'll need clothes to keep here anyway... if you want."

Her eyebrows raised while her lips pursed, "Ooo to keep here? I like the sound of that. Since we are officially boyfriend and girlfriend now. I wished I brought a suitcase when I saw how clean your place was. You never know with guys." She bumped his shoulder while standing up. "I'm excited lets go."

She took a deep breath as they walked past the red pillars into Target. "I love the smell of this place. It so amazing." While walking around, the basket became filled with leggings, hoodies, sports bras, two packs of underwear, a blanket, two romance novels, body wash, face cleanser and moisturizer, her favorite deep conditioner and curling crème.

Gemini was eyeing the bonnets and combs. "You don't need to buy a bonnet or anything. You can keep using the one I gave you."

She smiled up at him, "Cool! I forgot about that." When they arrived to the checkout counter, Calvin began loading everything. She couldn't help but to steal more than a few glances at his ass. She scanned her reward barcode and he paid. *Okay I can get used to this.*

When they went back to his place, she practically ran into his bathroom with the bags. She arranged her face and body wash in the shower and moisturizer on the counter. She has happy to invade his space. She turned on the shower and began playing some music. As she dried off and opened the door to the bedroom, Calvin was looking right at her on the bed.

"You look stunning Gemini," he said with an intensity that made her wet shoulders shiver.

"Thank you," she said with a sly smile. "You look damn good yourself. Thank you for the shopping trip." She bit her bottom lip and dropped the towel. His jaw dropped as he quickly stood up and walked towards her.

"You have to give me a heads up before doing that. If I stare at the sun for too long, I'll go blind." He leaned down and kissed her collar bone, up her neck to the bottom of her ear. Then he whispered, "If your face was the last one I ever saw, I would never complain in heaven because I saw an angel." He looked at her in the eyes again and lightly kissed her.

"Oh really?" she asked breathlessly. His arm wrapped around her lower back, his fingers brushing against her waist.

"Yes, really baby." Then he kissed her. Not like at the hotel, or even the night before. This kiss made her melt from her pinky toe, to the lower part of her neck. His arms were wrapped around her like they were in a black and white movie. They were on a cloud a foot off the ground. She thought he would dip her onto the floor. As their tongues brushed against each other, her hands grabbed onto the lower part of his shirt and lifted it over his head. His chest hot against her cold nipples. Their moaning grew louder as she began to push Calvin towards the bed.

Chapter Fifteen

Gemini

When Gemini woke up from her post sex nap, Calvin was lying next to her watching TV in the bedroom. "You're awake," he said with a smile. "You are so beautiful when you first wake up."

She blinked a few times stretching, "Thank you. How long was I out for?"

"Not long, Greg will be here in an hour to drop off the order and stay for a session. Are you comfortable with that?"

She sleepily nodded. "Yea this is your place, why are you asking me permission?"

"Because I want to make sure you're comfortable." She smiled and kissed his lips. He had been nothing but considerate of her since they met. She was won over when he put her hair in a bonnet for her.

She rolled out of bed. "Okay. I'm going to take another shower and this time I'm going to stay clean. I don't want to smell like sex when he gets here. A first impression is everything."

He held his hands up. "Will do, I'll behave."

She swallowed her gasp when Greg walked through the door. He was easily 6'2" wearing a red T shirt and black joggers, his chest and gut pronounced. *Fuck a dad bod, so sexy.* His hair was in a short afro with a fresh line up. His beard was long and he was clean cut. His shoulders were wide and strong. She wanted to know what his hands looked like, felt like. *Omg you're Calvin's girlfriend now, you can't go after the best friend.* Calvin dapped Greg up as he took off his shoes. Of course two fine black men are friends. She couldn't decide who was finer.

Calvin was 5'9", with a slim muscular frame. He had his own way about him that just draws you in, with or without his glasses. Greg, off of first impression, was the guy girls flock to with his linebacker build. "Evening man," his voice was so baritone her heart pounded harder. Damn.

Calvin walked over to Gemini with a smile, "This is my girl Gemini. Gemini, this is my man Greg. We go way back." When Greg walked over to her and shook her hand, just the smell of his cologne turned her on even more.

"Hi," was all that came out of her mouth.

A half smile lifted on his lips, "Hey gorgeous, you're even more beautiful in person". He eyed her in a way that made her cross her legs when she really wanted to open them. She had to look away, was she blushing? He chuckled as he sat down on the couch.

"Greg, don't steal my girlfriend!" Calvin yelled from the kitchen. "She's a good one."

Greg chuckled, "We good bro. We just talking, right?"

He looked at her in the eye, she didn't realize that his eyes were a hazel brown until now. He smiled at her again. She found her voice, "Yep, all good over here babe." Calvin threw up a thumbs up.

"How did you end up with my boy Calvin?"

She tucked her braids behind her ears, playing with the ends with her hands. She glanced at Calvin, but his back was turned. Why did she want both? She's Calvin's girlfriend, she is taken. "We met at the bar. I was reading and he asked about my book. Then it blossomed from there." She turned to look at Calvin, "He's been good too. I didn't know he could paint like this though." She pointed to the various art pieces around the living room.

Greg chuckled, "Yea I love his art. That shit is cool, but he never sells them. He hung a piece in the library, but he won't tell anyone which one or where it is. He says 'the real ones will see it.' Whatever that means."

Calvin began putting ashtrays on the side tables. "I'm about to roll up."

Greg dropped Gemini's order on the table and pulled a blunt out of his pocket. "I'll match."

"Oh shit let me get my wallet upstairs." Gemini quickly got up and ran upstairs, glad she had black leggings on because she was definitely wet. She was nervous to glance down the stairs to see Calvin and Greg looking up at her, staring at her ass. She grabbed the cash and quickly came down the stairs, her breast bouncing along the way.

As they were passing the blunt around, Gemini thought about what Greg said by being more beautiful in person. "Greg, what did you mean by 'in person' earlier? We've never met before so how did you see me?" She asked while blowing out smoke.

Greg and Calvin exchanged a look, a secret man look. "Uhh I don't wanna lie but I watched the camera footage of Calvin eating you out in the library awhile back. You still had most of your clothes on but uhh… it caught the audio."

Gemini's jaw hit the ground as she turned to Calvin. "Wow you weren't gonna say nothin?"

Calvin swallowed. "Sorry, but he did delete it." He smiled sheepishly. Gemini sighed, how could he not tell her someone else saw her up on that desk being devoured.

Wait.

But it was sexy ass Greg that saw them. Maybe it turned him on? This could be a way to smooth everything over and everyone be happy.

"Did you like the little movie Greg?" Gemini asked him, eyeing him up and down.

Greg coughed and exchanged another glance to Calvin. "Uhh I mean yea it was cool and a lil sexy. It was the noises you were making and all that."

Gemini smiled at them in a playful way as she tossed her

braids. "So I have a proposition then. Calvin, since you withheld this information from me. I think it's only fair that I have some fun with Greg, if he's okay with it."

Their eyes were wide as they glanced at each other. "Have some fun?" Calvin asked her.

"Like a threesome?" Greg asked.

"Only if you're up to it, since you have seen some of my goods already." She lightly brushed her hands against her legs.

Greg played with the collar on his shirt, he did have a girlfriend, so she understood if it was a hard no. He took out his phone and began texting.

Calvin stood up. "Can I talk to you for a second Gem?"

"Sure!" She squealed.

They went upstairs to his bedroom and closed the bedroom door. "What the hell Gemini? I just asked you out yesterday and you're trying to fuck my best friend?"

She put her finger in his face. "No, that's not what's happening. You have known, for days, that Greg saw the footage of us in the library. But for whatever reason, you didn't want to say a peep about it. To me, withheld information is a lie. So, since he's already seen my pussy in the air. Greg can get a live view. You didn't even give me a heads up!"

Calvin paused and looked away, "So that's your justification?" He rubbed the back of his neck. "You're right.. you're right. We can do the threesome". He took a deep breath and looked at Gemini in the eye. "I have to tell you something else while we're here. I have a crush on Greg and I have for awhile, like years."

Gemini giggled quietly. "I mean he is fine I get it. I don't know how you expected me to act. But he is not what I was imagined when you mentioned 'your friend Greg.'"

"He's a Leo so he does have a way of claiming a room. Let's do it."

As they walked back down the stairs, Greg held up his phone. "I got permission from bae, so I'm good as long as we use condoms."

Gemini looked over at Calvin. She grabbed his collar and pulled him into her. He seemed surprised by the kiss, but Gemini couldn't hold it. As Gemini bit Calvin's bottom lip, she looked over at Greg. She stared into his eyes as she continued to kiss Calvin, Greg stared back eying her body. She waved her index finger over for Greg to come over.

He smiled as he stood up and sat closer to her. She stopped kissing Calvin and whispered in his ear, "Is it okay if I kiss him?" Gemini stroked his ear with her index finger. Calvin nodded with hooded eyes.

Gemini leaned back and kissed Greg, her hand rested on his strong jaw. Calvin's hands rubbed and squeezed her thighs and Greg's rough hand cradled her neck. She lifted her leg over Calvin's legs as his hands began massaging her inner thigh. She put her hand on Greg's chest for balance and to remind herself this was reality. Gemini could feel Greg's chest rising and falling faster as their tongues met. She couldn't wait to see what he looked like without clothes.

Calvin was drawing circles in between the seams in her leggings, making her legs twitch as her tongue danced on Greg's.

Her heart was beating so fast that she couldn't hold in her moans. Greg's hands began massaging Gemini's stomach and sides. She lifted his hand to her breast. He gently began playing with her nipples as Calvin began pulling down her leggings.

Gemini quickly lifted her shirt over her head as Calvin pulled the leggings off her. The cold air made her shiver. "Don't worry we'll keep you warm," Greg said in her ear. He softly kissed her ear lobe as he rubbed his hands up her arms and down her chest. Gemini looked at Calvin as he admired her, the sexual intensity growing in his eyes.

"You know we will baby," Calvin hummed as he kissed the gaps between her breast, down her stomach to her hips and down her thighs. Gemini felt like she could burst from the attention she was getting. She wanted to be filled with both of them, but only one had her heart. She stood up, the men looked up at her.

She waved her index finger to Greg and he stood up behind her. Gemini stood in front of Calvin as she danced on Greg, swaying her hips against him. He matched her pace and caught everything she was throwing back. She played with her nipples as she looked down at Calvin, Greg's hands squeezed her hips as he groaned behind her. When she bent over to kiss to Calvin, Greg smacked her bare ass and squeezed. A small yelp escaped her lips, then a wide grin. As Gemini and Calvin kissed deeper, Greg massaged her ass, spread her lips and slowly rubbed her clit. Her knees buckled as he went faster and faster. Gemini's hands felt on Calvin's length as her rise began to grow.

Gemini pulled back from kissing Calvin as Greg's finger entered her wet palace. "Fuck," she groaned. Calvin kissed her cheek and down her neck.

"Finish baby, be my good girl and come on Greg's hand. You know you want to." Calvin whispered as he looked into her eyes. Her eyes squeezed shut as she came, the sound of her sweetness filled the room. A ripple shocked her whole body and almost knocked her off balance.

Greg licked his finger, "One down, many to go baby."

"Don't you think we would be more comfortable in the bedroom?" She began slowly walking towards the stairs. As they watched her, confidence grew even more inside of her. She craved this feeling of being in control. "Why am I the only one moving? Take your clothes off." Calvin and Greg pushed each other as they started moving towards the stairs. Before Gemini made it to the top, the pair were only in their boxers, right behind her.

She glided into Calvin's room and turned on the blue lights. They sat on the edge of the bed, never taking their eyes off her. But Calvin's eyes gleamed with more passion... for her. Gemini climbed towards the pillows, her skin glowing blue like mermaid scales as she began lightly massaging her breast in front of them. Greg extended his hand towards her ankle, but she pulled it away. "Did I ask you to touch me? Calvin, your friend here needs to learn about me and the rules here." Greg's eyes widen as Calvin's eyes were soft, waiting for her.

Gemini eyed them both, "You don't move unless I tell you too. How obedient can you be Greg?"

Greg looked at Calvin and back at her. "I can be obedient." His dark chocolate skin gleaming under the blue light surrounding the room. Even though he stood a head taller than Calvin, she still wondered whose dick would be bigger.

"Calvin sit to my right, Greg you're on my left." They sat down on both sides of her. She leaned to her left and began kissing Greg again. Her left hand brushed Greg's chest while her right hand went into Calvin's boxers. Calvin kissed her shoulder, across her chest and licked her nipple. She dug her nails into Greg's chest as they moaned. "Take your boxers off," she whispered. They both stood up and took their boxers off.

She leaned back on the bed, "Calvin, I want you to fuck my face as Greg eats me out."

As Calvin crawled on top of her, Greg was spreading her legs. As Calvin filled Gemini's mouth, she filled Greg's. Her hands rested firmly on Calvin's waist as she sucked his dick. Her throat full of him as drool fell from the corner of her lips. As she slowly worked her hands to his ass, he groaned louder above her. Her thumb teasing his hole while he stroked her wet lips.

As Greg slipped in two fingers, her back began to arch. He twisted his fingers against her clit, his tongue flat against her folds. Greg increased his speed as she began slowing down, licking Calvin up to his head. "Where's the condoms?" Greg asked.

"Top drawer to the left," Calvin said in-between grunts. She felt Greg move from the bed and watched him grab the gold packets.

Gemini lightly pushed Calvin back and took a deep breath. "Need some help?" She asked Greg.

He was already jacking himself off as she crawled to the foot of the bed. She waved her finger over to Greg and watched him walk over. She put all of him in her mouth. Greg's hand squeezed her shoulder as she continued. *Calvin was definitely the winner of the size war.*

Then Calvin came behind her, kissing the back of her thigh, up to her ass and back. Gemini's heart began to race as he lifted her hips in the air, entering her as she groaned against Greg's pelvis. Her hands massaging his balls and sensitive gap. Greg cursed above her as Calvin got deeper inside of her. His force so hard that it made Gemini deep throat Greg.

No complaints on her end.

As Gemini was sucking on Greg's tip, she looked up and saw how they looked at each other. Greg was enjoying her tongue as Calvin stroked her slowly, but their eyes were glued to each other. They were having their own moment too. Gemini released Greg with a *pop* that made him whimper, "Yall can kiss, if you want." They paused and looked at each other. Gemini could read the history and tension in their bodies. Greg brushed his thumb across Calvin's cheek, while Calvin hungrily stared at his lips.

The men crashed into each other like a wave.

Gemini moved out of the way and watched them. Greg kissed Calvin from the side of his jaw, down his neck and chest to his tip. Calvin's head tossed back in pleasure as his hands explored Greg's solid frame. As Greg pushed Calvin's dick deeper in his mouth, a loud groan escaped both of them. He sucked Calvin it in a way that made her jealous. She couldn't stop pleasuring herself, massaging her clit listening to Greg devour Calvin. She looked up at Calvin's face, his mouth slightly open with his teeth clenched together.

He was getting close.

As Calvin's hand was behind Greg's head, she got up and began kissing him. His head fell back as he groaned even louder in her mouth as she squeezed his ass. "I'm gonna come fuck," Calvin gasped. Greg moved faster and faster until the veins started showing in Calvin's neck as he came on Greg's lips. As he stood up to wash his face, Gemini sucked the rest off. Calvin was at a loss for words.

When Greg came back into the room, Gemini called him back to the bed. He came and wrapped his arm around her waist. She leaned and whispered in his ear, "Now it's your turn to finish." She began to massage his length as he looked her in the eye.

"Damn." Greg said with a grunt.

She smiled at him. "Are you enjoying yourself?"

"Yea yea I am," she leaned back and sat up, "Fuck me."

Greg grabbed the condom and prepared himself as Gemini crawled to the top of the bed, leaned back on the pillows and gently brushed her thighs while looking at them. As Calvin kissed her ankle, Greg sucked her. "Mmm you taste good baby," Greg moaned as he dived deeper into her.

Gemini began to squirm, then Calvin's voice was in her ear, "Be a good girl and keep taking it. Let that come go baby." He kissed her ear lobe.

"Ah fuck," she breathed as Greg's mouth devoured her. She

squeezed the back of his neck as she came on his mouth. She couldn't wait to feel his strength against her. "Fuck me, don't make me wait."

They chuckled, as Greg said, "As you wish."

He finished with a loud slurp and climbed on top of her. They moaned together as Greg entered her. She looked at Calvin with hooded eyes, as Greg pushed himself deeper and deeper inside her.

Greg lifted one ankle as Calvin lifted the other. As Greg's strokes slowed, Calvin began rubbing his head against her clit. Feeling both of their dicks tease her sent her into a frenzy. She bit down hard on her bottom lip, looking into their eyes as they drank her in.

Greg then shoved himself deeper, making her yelp. "Oh you're still not done coming yet. Turn around."

She lifted herself and turned around, resting on her forearms. Her thighs shook as she arched her back. Then Calvin and Greg took turns fucking her as she screamed, moaning and moving her hips against them.

Every time they switched, she bit the pillow harder because they pounded with more strength than the last. Greg pulled out and came into the condom with a loud grunt. Gemini threw herself down on the bed, her hips throbbing of pleasure. Her body falling into a restful shock. Calvin gently brushed his hands lightly against her skin, from her wrist to her shoulder and neck. "How do you feel?" He asked her breathlessly.

"Fucking amazing," she took a deep breath. "I need to take

a shower."

Calvin kissed her back, "Go ahead baby."

She slowly rolled out of the bed and limped in the shower. When she came out, Calvin and Greg were laying on the bed entwined together. Their chocolate skin melting into each other as their hands covered their bodies. It gave Gemini goosebumps watching their facial expressions.

She didn't know if Calvin would notice her. She stood in the bathroom doorway watching them in her towel, drinking in every moment they made against each other. Then, Calvin stood up and grabbed her hand.

"Are you ready to call it a night baby?" Calvin asked her.

Gemini nodded. Calvin opened his drawers and handed her one of his t-shirts and the bonnet. She quickly slipped it on. Greg stood up, "Imma grab my clothes from downstairs and head out. But damn I've always wanted to do that Calvin, but I never thought we would. I'm glad we did." He left the room and closed the door behind him. When they heard the front door close, Calvin went downstairs to lock the door and brought up some bottles of water.

Gemini's body was still vibrating from the experience. It felt like her skin was glowing as a cozy feeling filled her. He handed her the bottle of water as she leaned against the wall. "Do you want to sleep in my guestroom? It can be a nice change of scene and the sheets are clean."

She sleepily chucked, "That's perfect."

Calvin grabbed her hand, kissed her knuckles, and guided

her to the guestroom. When they got into the bed, she laid her head on his chest, snuggling closer to him in the cool sheets. His arms rested around her body. She loved wearing his clothes and taking in his smell. There was no better feeling than hearing his heartbeat as her head rested on him. She didn't feel insecure about the moments between him and Greg.

They were friends after all and Greg had a girlfriend. Bi black men exist and it's okay for them to be with whoever they choose. She was glad Calvin told her about his feelings for Greg beforehand. That took maturity and honesty. He kissed her forehead, as whispered "Good night baby," rubbing her back as she drifted off to sleep.

Chapter Sixteen

Calvin

Calvin waved at security as he walked into the Grant Enterprises' Corporate building, the main headquarters of his family's business. He had a fun weekend, especially with him and Gemini's escapades with Greg. While driving, his mind would drift to the look on Gem's face, the taste of Greg's face. That was the best experience he'd ever had. As he walked the usual path headed to the CEOs office, his moms old office that's now his sisters, all he could think about was the face Coraline made when the news broke. It was like she saw a ghost.

He knocked on the glass door and walked in. Coraline was sitting with her head in her hands, her shoulders hunched over shivering. "Are you crying?" he quietly asked, closing the door behind him.

She looked up at him surprised with red teary eyes and scoffed. "Me cry? Get real." She sniffled and turned her head away, a tissue already in her hand. He sat down in the black chair in front of her desk. He couldn't imagine what she was going through in the new position already. He watched her as more tears began to well up in her eyes, even though she poorly fought them off. He sat silently until he couldn't anymore.

"So, do you want to talk about it? Or just badly hold it in until you have a real breakdown."

She sighed as she stood up and looked out of her office window that overlooked busy streets below and the Atlanta skyline. "Do you remember mom's old apartment? The one we grew up in."

He nodded. "Yes, I do remember. It wasn't the best but it was what we had at the time."

She looked down out of the window again, her arms crossed. "There were things that happened in that apartment that I'll probably never talk about... But to go from there to here. It just feels like I'm not supposed to be here you know? I knew mom was training me the whole time. I'm the oldest. I've been sitting in meetings with her since I was at least 12, maybe younger."

"I was 10." Calvin chimed. She turned and looked at him with her arms crossed. "Sorry, continue."

"But now her office is mine and it's weird. I remember when we moved into this building, and she chose this office because it had the best view. Now I'm the CEO of Grant Enterprises before I'm even 30? Everything is really on me now. I'm used to being micromanaged and running everything through mom and now she isn't here. What if I fuck up? Who do I go to for advice now?" Coraline put her head in her hand again.

"She'll still be there to answer questions and guide you. But, you also worked damn hard to get here Coraline. Nobody knows the business better than you. You and Casey both are the roots of this business. You've been doing Moms job ever since you could." He stood up and grabbed her hands, they were shaking. "You definitely deserve to sit in that seat, Mom's *old* seat. I'm genuinely proud of you for how you've held everything together."

Coraline's eyes welled up again. She pulled him in for a hug. It surprised him but he hugged her back. Usually, a hair was never out of place on her head. She never showed weakness in public or private spaces. But she needed her little brother. He was glad he came to check on her.

She sniffled again, "You are making me ruin my make up."

"No you were crying when I got here." They laughed. Casey walked into the office.

"Aww did I miss a lil family moment? Group hug!" Casey skipped up to them and wrapped them in a big hug. Calvin rolled his eyes and hugged his sisters. Even though he was sometimes forgotten, he wouldn't change his family.

When they released, Casey punched Calvin arm, "So when are you bringing your girlfriend over to meet us? If she's even real."

He crossed his arms, "I'm scared that if she meets the both of you she'll run."

They gasped, "Lies"! Coraline said. "I would just interview her about her personal and work history. Do some background check digging."

"I'll be good! I'm the chill one remember" Casey chimed.

He took his phone out of his pocket, "Fine, I'll invite her to dinner. You don't think it's too early? I just asked her to be my girlfriend last weekend."

"No," they chimed together. Coraline went back to the desk and opened a drawer. She took out a pocket mirror, several Fenty products and began fixing her make up while simultaneously typing on her laptop.

"Well, I have a meeting in a few minutes. Some of us have jobs to do."

Calvin smiled. "And *The Woman King* is back." He dusted off his shirt, "I have saved the day again. See yall on Sunday." His sisters rolled their eyes as he exited the office. He was actually nervous about inviting Gemini over for dinner. What if it went wrong? But everything could also go perfect.

He called her and she answered on the second ring, "Hello!" her voice sang in his ear.

He grinned. "Hey hey! Is now a good time?"

He heard birds chirping in the back ground of her line. "Yea I'm on my lunch break so I'm sitting outside. What's up?"

Calvin took a deep breath as he got in his car. "How would you feel about coming to dinner with me on Sunday? Well with me to meet my family."

Gemini gasped. "I get to meet the Grant clan? I'd love too! That sounds like fun. I'm not doing anything. I'm looking forward to meeting them."

His stomach warmed. She's looking forward to it. "Great! I'll pick you up at 11."

Gemini squealed, "Awesome! I can't wait to meet your sisters."

He smiled into the phone, "They can't wait to meet you either."

Her voice started to crack, "You've told them about me already?"

"Of course I have. I told them about you the Sunday after we met. You were on my mind too much. I was scared I ruined everything for coming on too strong." He cleared his throat. "Does that make me weird?"

She laughed. "I appreciate you telling me that. I was wondering if you did. No it doesn't make you weird. It's been over a month since then." She said chuckling. "I'll see you on Sunday."

"See you then Gem."

Chapter Seventeen

Gemini

Calvin downplayed the size of his mother's house. The driveway was a long stretch, with two other cars parked in front of theirs. The mansion was breathtaking. "Sir, why did you not tell me we were pulling up to Uncle Phil and thems house? This home is literally beautiful. Shit it's big."

"Yea, she moved on up from East Point. Casey was too young to remember our old apartment. So she got to grow up in this house, go to this school district, so she was raised a little different than Coraline and I. "

"You must be jealous." He shrugged at her as she stared at the home.

As they walked up to the front door, Calvin was staring at Gemini with that inquisitive look again. She glanced at him quick enough to catch it while admiring the hedge the lined the walkway. "Why are you looking at me like that again?" She said while playing with her dress, letting it flow and dance around her legs.

She decided an emerald-green sundress would be the most

appropriate attire. "You look beautiful, especially in emerald." He said with a wide smile. He knocked at the door and began turning the key, "Here we go."

Gemini grinned as she walked into the entryway. There was a nice table with a large mirror, close to the door. Then the walkway opened into a small sitting area, then the room extended to the large living room and dining room. Her breath was taken away. A very tall woman came around the corner with an ankle length black dress with a blue cardigan. Her face was serious, but then lifted into a smile when they made eye contact.

Her features were sharp and feline like, while her eyes were a light brown. She was slim and had a beautiful long neckline. "This must be Gemini," the woman said in a TV anchor, professional voice. "How are you? I'm Coraline."

Gemini smiled, "Hi! It's so nice to meet you." Coraline hugged her shoulders then walked over to Calvin.

"You didn't tell us she was this beautiful little brother". Coraline punched his shoulder, and he gave her a look. "How and where did you all meet? This guy never leaves the library."

Calvin's face scrunched together, so Gemini decided to answer with a charming grin. "I was reading at a bar, and he approached me. After I finished reading of course, like a true gentleman." He smiled back at her.

"Of course you're a book nerd sweetheart. He's been obsessed with books as long as I can remember. Anyways, Casey is here already and Mama's finishing up in the kitchen. So make yourselves comfortable, wash your hands and meet us in the dining room."

She tossed another smile towards Gemini and went back into the living room. Calvin placed his hand on her back. "It's alright, they don't bite." He guided her to the guest bathroom and they washed their hands.

When she stepped out into the hallway, a younger woman came out of nowhere and hugged Gemini. She was a few inches shorter than her and had wide hips and thighs. Her long black hair waved past her butt. She wore a light pink floral romper "Ahh girl you are so fine! I love your braids sis! I'm Casey. I've heard SO many things about you." Casey ran her hand through Gemini's braids and tapped her shoulder.

Gemini blushed. "I hope all good things."

Casey laughed while lopping in her arm with hers. "Of course! We had to give Calvin a little push to make sure he didn't fuck things up." She looked back at Calvin. His face was in his hand. As they walked to the dining room, Casey led her to a seat and Calvin sat on the other side of her.

Then his mother appeared, "Oh! You must be Gemini, Calvin told us we should be expecting his girlfriend." As Gemini stood up as his mom, ran over.

"Don't move honey I'll come to you." She hugged her from behind and kissed her cheek. She smelled like fresh vanilla.

"Thank you for having me Ms. Grant." The scent of fried chicken and greens were making her mouth water and stomach grumble. Coraline and Casey came and placed the serving dishes at the center of the table. They brought out a plate of chicken, bowls of collard greens and rice, okra, cornbread and corn.

After Calvin prayed over the food, everyone began to fix their plates. Gemini silently passed the bowls around and fixed her plate. Then she noticed the jazz music playing in the background. *Say something, you're being too quiet.* "I see where Calvin gets his love of jazz music from." Gemini said smiling looking around the table, searching for acknowledgement.

Ms. Grant nodded her head along the music, "With the industry we work in, well that I used to work in." Ms. Grant smiled widely at Coraline as she gave a forced smile back. "I have learned to value slow music. Back in my day on the pole-", the siblings groaned together.

Gemini's head turned to the side, "Huh on the pole? I thought your family business was in finance?" She said turning to Calvin.

Everyone's neck broke to look at Gemini, then to Calvin and back at her. Then Casey spoke, "Girl we own bars and clubs, like strip clubs, titty bars," Casey said while twerking in her seat. "I'm the executive trainer, for the dancers and Coraline is the new CEO."

Calvin's eyes stayed down as Coraline spoke. "Grant Enterprises owns multiple high grossing establishments, like bars and clubs, across the country. Our mother started it and worked very hard to get it where it is today. Calvin didn't tell you what we, really manage, huh? Sounds like him." Coraline shot him a cold look. "He loves keeping information to himself, typical." He swallowed his food harder, gripping his fork.

Gemini stared at the side of Calvin's head trying to not slap him. She felt stupid. Why did he tell her finance when they met?

That's a stupid thing to lie about.

Why wasn't he speaking up? He had shut down right in front of her and his family wasn't helping the situation either. "Can you excuse us for a second? Calvin, can you walk me to the car real quick?"

He nodded and stood up, stuffing his hands in his pocket as he followed her out. She wanted to grab him by the shirt collar and drag him out. But she didn't. When they made it outside, she crossed her arms and stood next to the car. The Atlanta sun already resting on her arms. He still couldn't lift his head.

"So you won't even look at me?" He rocked back and forth. "Okay then. So were not going to talk about how I got embarrassed back there because you lied to me about something small?"

"I'm sorry. I di-didn't tell you. I don't like to tell folks about what my fam does cause then they ask questions, ask about my sisters and-." He turned away, his face hardened. "There's some weird people out there. So, I don't tell anyone. It keeps them safe, so finance it is."

She sighed, pressing her lips together. She understood what he meant about wanting to protect his family. It is his family's business. He didn't have to tell her everything, but she thought he trusted her more. She grabbed his hand and he stopped rocking. "Can you look at me?" she asked. He looked up at her, deep in the eyes. His searching chocolate eyes stared back at her. "I understand wanting to keep your family safe. But you invited me to meet your family. You still could've given me a heads up on the way here or something. I care about getting to know you, the real you."

He squeezed her hand back. "You are right about that. I do apologize. I won't lie to you again." While maintaining her eye contact he brought her hands to his lips and kissed her palms. The anger that was growing in her chest was starting to dissipate onto the concrete, sizzing from the Georgia sun. Why did he have to be so sweet and secretive?

She couldn't hide her blush. "I hate when you do that."

"Do what?" She leaned and kissed his cheek.

"Make me melt." She chuckled. "Are there any other skeletons in the closet that I need to be made privy too? A secret child? Nothing else?"

He chuckled as she dropped her hands. "Not that I can think of right now."

"Mmhm. Good, come on then."

They walked back inside to finish dinner. The air conditioning was a cool blessing. It was weird, but she was more curious about their business. Gemini went to a pole dancing class a while ago and had the time of her life, she wished she stuck with it.

As Calvin and his sisters were in the kitchen cleaning, Gemini went outside. Ms. Grant was sitting with her feet in the pool, looking across their beautiful, manicured backyard. "May I join you?" Gemini asked.

Ms. Grant patted the stone next to her. Gemini slid off her shoes, grabbed the bottom of her dress, kneeled down and put her feet in the pool. The sun sat on her skin, but the cool water calmed her body. They sat there quietly next to each other for a few moments.

"How are you enjoying retirement so far Ms. Grant?"

"It's bittersweet dear." She took a deep breath, it looked like memories passed in front of her. "I'm glad I don't have meeting after meeting. The flying around the country was fun when I was younger, but it gives me a headache now. I do miss working with my children. My daughters have done an excellent job of maintaining my work. I was 25 when I bought the club I worked in. They looked at me like I was crazy. But I made everybody more money.

"The game is a bit different now. Casey wants to do her own thing. I had the same passion at her age. That's what eventually brought us here." Ms. Grant waved her hand around the pool and towards the mansion behind her. "I've done my job, built my legacy and took care of my family. Now, I can rest. I'm looking forward to that. It's been a long time since I could do whatever I wanted."

Gemini looked at her feet under the water. It made her reflect on her own life. Even though she was only 28, she wanted to be on the path to growth and retirement at the reasonable age. She never gave it much thought but she could have a family. Would it be crazy to say she could imagine her and Calvin's kids running thought this same backyard? "I do wish you congratulations still. I know we just met, but I'm proud of you."

Ms. Grant turned and looked at her and smiled. "Thank you, sweetheart. Pardon my French, but I hope Calvin doesn't fuck things up with you. I like you. He's different from his sisters, but I love them all the same." They laughed together and they heard the back door close. Gemini really enjoyed listening to Ms. Grant.

"Can you tell me more about when you used to dance?"

A wide grin grew on Ms. Grant's face. "Oh, girl I was a sight. I can still do a thing or two," she lowered she shades and raised her eyebrows. Gemini's laugh roared.

"Uh oh if y'all are laughing it can't be good." Gemini turned around and smiled, looking up at Calvin.

"Your mom is hilarious and very wise. Ms. Grant, would you mind if we hung out more? We don't need a chaperone," pointing at Calvin.

As Ms. Grant laughed, Calvin gasped. "Mama you not about to steal my woman."

"What can I say? I have that effect on people." It had been so long since Gemini was around a family unit. She was happy Calvin opened that door to let her in. Even though he lied, she understood where he was coming from. Her eyes were open and she was enjoying seeing Calvin's layers. As Gemini looked around, she didn't feel like a stranger. She felt like she had known them for years, even though they met today. She hoped it wasn't her last time here.

Chapter Eighteen

Calvin

Calvin looked out of the back window, watching Gemini sit with his mom warmed his heart. He knew he made a good choice bringing her around. Yes, he should've given her a heads up about what the family business really was. Yes, he fucked up again. But damn. Seeing how the sun danced on her body, her feet playing in the water. She was meant to be in his life. She blended into his life so well. He wanted her to stay forever.

As they were walking towards the door, Gemini hugged Casey and Coraline. Ms. Grant kissed her cheek. "Calvin, you be good. Well try your best."

They laughed. When they got closer to the door, Gemini groaned to herself. "What? What's wrong baby?"

She sighed. "I have to take out my hair tonight. So I'm preparing my shoulders for the task."

"I can help. Let me take your hair out and wash your hair." She gave him a confused look. Her eyebrows and mouth twisted.

"Help me with my hair? No it's okay. I can do it myself."

Casey's voice called from the living room. "Trust him girl! He's done all of our hair before. Twists, cornrows, silk press, box braids and all." It was true. Appearance has always been a big thing in the family. So he watched tapes, sat in some hair salons, *more like went to Mama and Coraline's hair appointments,* to observe technique and tried different styles on his sisters' hair.

He knew he was getting good when Mama asked him to flat iron her hair before leaving for work at night. There was a small part of him that missed wrapping his sisters' hair before bed.

Gemini's jaw dropped. "Oh wow yall not lying?"

The voices of all three women said, "No we're not." He shrugged his shoulder and pouted his lips.

Gemini gave him a look that made his body feel weak. He needed to bring her home as soon as possible. The quicker he started, the quicker he would be finished. "Alright y'all bye!" He and Gemini waved goodbye as he closed and locked the door behind them.

As he drove on 285, he rested his hand on her thigh, brushing his thumb as her hand rested on top of his. She was reading her book out loud, just enough for him to hear her. He never wanted her to get behind the wheel again. There was something about how the light hit her round glossed lips, her warm calming voice. He was glad when they hit traffic because he could stare at her, undisturbed.

Then her voice paused, "We need to go by the hair store."

"Why? You already bought hair stuff for my place." A wide smile spread across her face. They did go on a *Target* adventure.

"Oh yea I forgot. Thank goodness we thought ahead. Do you have combs and all that?"

He nodded, trying to forget why he had the proper combs already. "Yea got that covered."

As they took out Gemini's braids, they binged watched *Legendary*. She was sitting on the floor, as Calvin worked from above. Her sitting in between in his legs, sitting on a pillow. He was also excited to see her natural curls for the first time. Was her hair dyed red or were the braids just red? He was curious to know.

After Gemini's hair was out, he messaged her scalp with his fingers and knuckles. "Finally," she moaned. "Thank you so much for your help." She stood up and stretched. "Now I'll just wash it and detangle it." She groaned heading up the stairs.

"Can I wash your hair?"

She turned, "Wash my hair? Like shampoo, condition, the whole works too?"

He chuckled, "Yes baby. I want to take care of you."

She smiled. "Well join me in the shower then." They began taking their clothes off as he followed her to her bathroom.

Chapter Nineteen

Gemini

Is this man really massaging my scalp while my deep conditioner is setting in? Yes, he is. Wherever Calvin came from, needs to be celebrated. She couldn't understand how he could be so forceful and aggressive in bed, but gentle as his fingers ran through her product drenched hair. He carefully ran his fingers through her curls to detangle and evenly spread the product. After 30 minutes, he rinsed it.

After he detangled and twisted her hair, it was past 10pm. "Do you want to stay here or go home? It's getting pretty late and I don't want you driving with the crazy's."

She stood up, stretched and kissed his cheek. "Okay I can stay but I have work tomorrow."

"How much do you make an hour?"

Her face scrunched. That's personal. What was he going to ask for next, her pay stub? "Why is that information important to you?"

"Because I want to know." He looked at her with his sincere

deep brown eyes and she folded. She couldn't say no to him if she tried. Not with the way he turned her into a puddle.

Gemini crossed her arms, "About $25 an hour." Calvin wiped his hands and began typing on his phone. Suddenly, a notification went off on her phone.

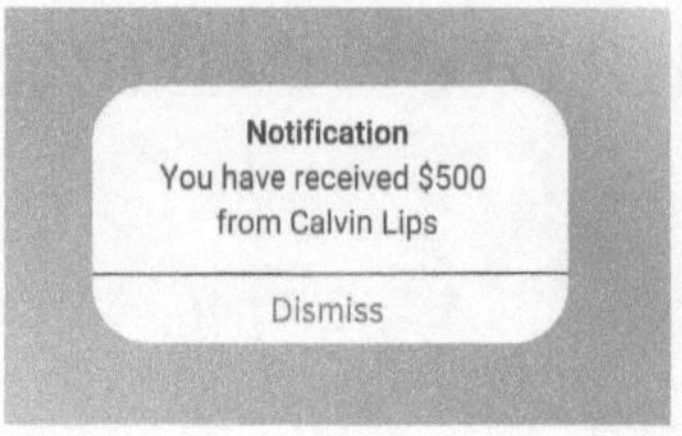

"Umm Calvin did you just send me money?"

He chuckled, putting his phone in his pocket. "Yes, I did."

"You didn't have to do that."

He chuckled. "Yes, I did. Call out of work tomorrow, I got you."

Her eyebrows raised so fast it almost gave her a headache. She was not used to this at all, even after the shopping trip. So, she texted her boss saying she wasn't feeling well and wouldn't be in.

Her boss responded 2 minutes later with a yellow thumbs up emoji. She rarely called out so she got grace, or she would find out when she went back to work. "Well, I officially won't be in tomorrow, so you've got me for a while."

Calvin licked his lips at her in a way that made her thighs jump. "Excellent, now I can have you all to myself." He walked towards her and she dove into his arms. As they kissed with their lips sliding against each other, happiness oozed out of her in more ways than one. The way his hands caressed her back and ass made her want to tear his clothes to shreds.

She bent her head down and bit his neck. "You keep waking up things up inside me baby."

"I never want to rest when I'm around you. I'm always going to give what you need and more baby." That made her heart beat even faster. They didn't stop kissing as he slowly carried her up the stairs.

Gemini limped to her car and exhaled. She was starting to get used to being around Calvin. Being away from him was starting to become boring. Call her crazy, but she was ready to move in with him, slowly but surely. His place was organized and so clean. Her lease was up in her apartment in a few months anyway. She had to call Serena for an update.

"Hey it's Serena."

"Bitch I have so much to update you on." She told Serena about the 'Gregscapade' and meeting his family.

"Ooo so you're pouring hot tea in my cup today! This is so sexy I love this for you. You really finessed a threesome, that's my girl. Who was bigger?

"Calvin was *technically* bigger, but Greg was thick as fuck. I was like damn okay fuck me then."

They laughed, "Wait you said something about a bonnet."

"Yea he gave me a bonnet my first night here and I've been using it ever since." Serena paused in a way that made Gemini worried. "You're thinking, I can tell. What are you thinking about?"

"Well, I don't want to press it. But did he used to have long hair or something? I've never heard of a guy having an extra bonnet laying around that wasn't their girls. Do you know if it was his?"

Gemini's stomach dropped. She didn't even think about who the owner of the bonnet was. She assumed it was him. She's been in the fog of sex and love, no questions came to mind. She could tell a woman used live there. "You know, I have no idea. Let me call him and see."

"Bet hit me back, I love you sis!"

"I love you too!"

Gemini gripped her steering wheel as she drove home, the tears began to fill her eyes. She had to confirm. Where did the fucking bonnet come from? There's no way he bought it for her before she got there. When she parked her car, she sat in the driver's seat and called him. "Hey baby, how are you?" he answered nonchalantly.

"Where did the bonnet come from?" she said coldly. Her hands were starting to shake as her eyes began to well.

"What?" Calvin said groggy and confused. "What bonnet?"

Of course, he's acting like he doesn't remember. "The bonnet you gave me the first night I went to your house. The bonnet

I wore every night when I stayed this weekend. Where did the bonnet come from?"

He grunted. "It was my ex's, she left it before she moved out."

What the fuck?

Her heart was beating out of her chest, "Before she moved out? How long ago were yall together? When did she move out?" This is the first time he's mentioned any ex-girlfriend.

He sighed, "We were together for three years. She used to work in the family business and that's that. Me and her broke up a month before we met."

Her stomach was doing summersaults. Three years. Three fucking years? He probably bought her a ring. That is a serious relationship. She knew a woman lived there, his house still looked like it. You can tell a women's touch on a house, on a man. He wasn't using three in one shampoo. "A month before? I thought you said it was awhile before you approached anyone at the bar."

"It had been."

"But you lied to me! Again Calvin! How dare you give me your ex's bonnet? Why did you keep it?"

"This is why I didn't want to talk about this ex shit bruh."

Gemini's face and hands got hot. Her teeth grinding into each other. "What? Yo watch how you talk to me Calvin. Don't curse at me!"

"You're over there trippin about a damn bonnet. Like what

the fuck Gemini? It wasn't like you brought one to use. I was just trying to look out for you."

"Because I didn't plan on staying over. That was the whole reason we went to Target. I feel so fucking stupid."

"Gem."

"No Calvin I'm good. Don't worry about me. You lied to me, a-fucking-gain. I shouldn't have to ask all these questions to get information out of you. I already gave you a chance to lay everything out to me and I'm only going so look like a fool so many times."

"Baby I-," *Click.* She knew she shouldn't have opened her heart again. What did Calvin do? Step on it. He tried to make it seem like she was overreacting when she wasn't. She didn't want to wear his exs fucking bonnet and he lied about when they broke up. Was she the rebound? Why did they break up and who broke up with who? All she had were questions that needed to be answered.

This was why she preferred to be alone. Why did Calvin have to pull these feelings out of her? Why did he have to look at her with those mahogany eyes? She put her phone in her purse and parked in her parking spot. Fuck everyone, and everything. Why did it seem like she only got answers when she asked questions? Why was he always so secretive? It doesn't take pulling teeth to get to know people. Right?

He asked her out but didn't give any more information about himself or his past. She must not have been asking enough.

No.

He didn't give enough, and she wasn't going to force it out of him either. Gemini was an inquisitive woman. It was part of her job to investigate things, review policies and listen to peoples problem to sort out the solution. She should've taken the hint when he lied about what his family did. She should've ran instead of talking it out.

She stomped her way up the stairs and kicked her apartment door open. Constance sleepily, raised her head then jumped down to greet her. She meowed and brushed her head against Gemini's leg. Gemini began to whimper. "He lied. He fucking lied again when he said he wouldn't. Everything must be a lie then. Why did I give him another chance?"

Constance blinked and licked her paw. Gemini threw herself on the couch and slumped. Constance brushed her head against Gemini's hand, looking at her with inquisitive eyes. She ran her fingers through her fur, taking deep breaths while the flood gates opened. What was the point of even trying anymore? She wasn't looking for someone. She just wanted to read at the bar in peace.

Fuck it.

She snatched her notebook and pen from the end table. She just drew circles and slowly pressed it further and further into the paper. Losing herself in the trance of the repetition.Then words came to mind. She slowly turned the page, the circle indents imprinted on the page. When the poem came, she let it flow.

The Cost
My time is longer with your dime
You're a pain, why did you lie?

I've been 100%
I even told you where I work at
We were just in Target shopping
You should've thrown a bonnet in that basket

For love language, you have to speak
You're meek
You're a coward
A fucking joke, bleak

You kept her stuff
There's a hold on you
When you held me, did you think about her?
Is that why you needed the family approval?

This is why I don't open up
I clam up and run
Like the hotel

You weren't worth my time
Or a damn
Fuck you

Calvin: Baby I'm sorry

Calvin: Please

Gemini woke up on the couch, she had a headache that sat behind her eyes. She was in no condition to go in the office. She knew her face was swollen. She grabbed her phone and rolled her eyes at the texts. It was 6:30pm on a freaking Monday. She called Serena back. "It was his ex's bonnet."

Serena gasped, the music turning down in the background. "I'm sorry. That's fucking weird. Why would he keep it?"

Gemini sniffled. "I don't know but I feel weird knowing it was hers. I guess she used to work with the family, they fell in love yada yada."

"Damn he didn't say nothing before today?"

Gemini wiped her nose as she sat up. "Nope. It should be against the law for men to have good dick." The tears began to well up in her eyes again, thinking about how his thumb brushed her cheek. The way his lips felt against hers. "Are you busy this week?"

Serena flipped papers in the background. "I think I can get away with working remote for a week. Need some girl time?"

"Yea, I need you." She swallowed the tears.

"Then I'm on my way. I'll send you my flight information."

Serena flew out to Atlanta on Tuesday morning. Even though their friendship was long distance, they could still count on each other. Gemini got approval to work from home for a week too. They both typed on their laptops while drinking coffee. Serena made breakfast, Gemini made lunch and they ordered take out for dinner.

Gemini was just happy she could hug her best friend and be in her presence. Being able to live in each others spaces for a week reminded them of college. The call volume was low so she could walk around the house with her headphones. As long as she answered emails and had a track of her work, Jane trusted her. Jane even emailed her a personal thank you for the service she provided to the CEOs office manager. She was glad to be recognized, from her boss. The weight of listening to people complain all day can take a toll on you.

When Friday night came, they threw the ultimate Self-care day. After they logged off work, they went to the gym to sweat out thoughts of Calvin. Nothing like running on a treadmill to get a man off of your mind. Gemini admired her figure when she returned home, she was mid-size and loved it. She never wanted to lose weight, but be more toned. She pinched her belly while turning to the side.

"Yes you are fine bitch! We thick." Serena pushed herself into the bathroom and shook her ass while sticking out her tongue out. Her blonde dreads shaking at her shoulders.

Gemini put her arm up and started twerking against the wall. "True! I'm fine and my friend fine ahh." After showering, they made natural face masks, listened to Summer Walker, smoked multiple blunts, ate ice cream and watched Waiting to Exhale. After the movie, they laid in bed together and stared at the ceiling.

"You know I love you right?" Gemini admitted to her.

Serena rolled her eyes, "Yes duh. Oh my god you're getting emotional." She rolled over and looked her in the eye. "You know I'll always be here when you need me, were sisters."

Gemini put her head against Serena's, "Thank you. I needed this. I just wasn't expecting any of this you know? I haven't been with someone in forever. So the fact Calvin opened the floodgate of feelings, it's hard to close back up."

"You know I understand. It was fucked up what he did. Has he tried to reach out?"

Gemini nodded. "Yea he used to blow my phone up. I couldn't bring myself to block his number. Then he just stopped… I think he got the hint."

Serena rubbed her shoulder. "It's okay, just take this time for you. You deserve the best and shouldn't settle. When you see red flags, it's okay to run. It's smarter."

"Yea," Gemini said with a sigh. She still missed him. His smell, the way his hands felt, how he looked while he read, his smile. A quiet sob escaped her as Serena rubbed her back. Constance jumped onto the bed and brushed her tail against Gemini's thigh as she settled into a ball.

Why wasn't she over him yet? Why was there a part of her that hoped he could get his shit together.

The next morning, Gemini held back her tears when she dropped Serena off at the airport. It was hard for both of them. It was like having a taste of home and peace.

Now it was back to the real world.

Chapter Twenty

Calvin

Calvin had felt sick ever since that phone call. She hadn't answered any of his calls or texts for the past week. He gave up on trying to get a response. He started stress cooking breakfast, pancakes, waffles, sausage, bacon and homemade orange juice. He was not in a good headspace. He had to think of a way to get her attention. He had to win her back. He didn't think the bonnet was that big of a deal. But he had to fix it. Which meant, doing a grand gesture.

Ring. The doorbell? He wasn't expecting anyone. Was it her? He looked through the peephole and saw Coraline. She had on a black short sleeve jumpsuit with her hair in a sleek high bun. Her black purse was rested in the crease of her arm wearing black shades to match. Her arms were crossed as she tapped her foot. He opened the door. "Well I have a visitor."

She took her shades off. "Hello little brother." He stepped out of the way and let her in. "Well how cozy. I love what you've done with the place. Your art has gotten better too."

Calvin eyed her. "Thanks."

She walked into the kitchen. "Expecting a crowd for breakfast?"

"No uh just a lot on my mind."

She opened the cabinet and grabbed a plate. Seeing Coraline move around his kitchen was… weird. What brought her to this side of town? "Well as you tell me everything, I'll fix my plate." She put two pancakes, a piece of sausage and a couple strips of bacon on her plate. Calvin looked at her as she poured the syrup. "I'm still waiting. I know it's about Gemini. You've got that heartbroken look in your eye again."

He sighed. "Yes, it's about Gemini. She hasn't been talking to me because I gave her you-know-who's bonnet when she stayed the night. She said I should've told her but it's just a bonnet right?"

Coraline's fork froze in the air. "What? So you're stupid, okay got it. I hope you were smart enough to at least wash it."

He rolled his eyes at her, "Yea I washed it. But it's not the end of the world, right? I don't want to lose her because of it. I just asked her to be my girlfriend and everything. I couldn't have fucked it up this soon."

Coraline cut her pancakes and put a fork full in her mouth and a sip of orange juice. "I see it from both sides. She wanted you to communicate something that you don't really care about." She took a bite of bacon. "You may not care, but she does brother. You also fucked up by withholding information. Are you embarrassed by what we do or something?"

He sighed, "When we were in high school, it got around that

mom used to dance. I got teased for it, a lot. Then they would make jokes about you and Casey following in her footsteps… niggas are gross and I hated that shit. So moving forward, I just said my family worked in finance so they would be out of my business."

Coraline looked him in the eye with understanding. "I get it. Those 'jokes' made their way to me too. It wasn't cool. But you can't bring that into your relationships Calvin. That was the past. Gemini wasn't even there. What's important to her, has to be important to you. To her, she wants to get to know you. The real you."

"Wow getting wisdom from my oh so wise sister, while she's eating my food."

Coraline took another bite of food. "Just like old times, right? You would cook, while I cleaned so mom wouldn't strangle us when she came home at 6am." They chuckled quietly.

He sighed. "I almost forgot about that."

"Yea. I could tell the stress on you while I pulled into the parking spot. You've always been a stress cooker." She grabbed another pancake. "I'm here to help you. Do you have any fruit?"

"Just some strawberries in the fridge." He zoned out, *strawberries*. The feel of her lips on the fruit. The taste of her skin while he licked the juices off of her. That was such an amazing night. He wanted to make her feel like a queen her first night.

"Ew are you thinking about her again? You're lovesick as fuck," she said with a laugh.

"Hey, keep it up or the kitchen will be closed."

She put her hands up. "Sorry, my compliments to the chef. Don't kick me out."

Calvin eyed her. "So what's the real reason for the visit? I can count on one hand the amount of times you've actually stepped foot in my house. After the contract was the signed."

Coraline sighed, her fork dancing on top of the soaked strawberry pancakes. "I want to work on getting closer to you."

Calvin gasped and put his hand on his heart. "Woah get closer? Are you okay? You eat like my sister, but she punches me to show affection not words."

"Look this is hard for me too short punk."

"There she is!" He yelled.

"Can you stop I'm trying to be serious. With mom stepping down that means, I'll need more help. I appreciated you coming by to check on me. I know you don't know a lot about the business. But-," she took another bite of food. Watching Coraline chew was giving Calvin heart burn. He was already surprised by her visit. She cleared her throat. "As hard as this is to admit. I need more help. At least a secretary or something. I'm starting to feel burned out planning and scheduling meetings while also preparing and presenting at them."

Calvin shrugged, "Have you talked to Casey?"

She gave him a look, "You know Casey likes to do her own thing. That's why we let her train. Did you know mom is letting her open her first pole studio here? So she'll be double booked now."

"Hmm," he said rubbing his chin.

"So I was thinking," she took another sip, her gulp echoing across the room. "How would you like to help me recruit and interview someone for the position? I at least need a secretary and business analyst for crunching numbers. I trust your judgement. You also haven't had any turnover at the library all year, that's impressive."

He pressed his lips together. "Coraline, have you been running reports and metrics on my staff again?"

She coughed. "What? No of course not. I visit, I just only go when you're not working?"

His eyebrows raised, "Really? Why have you never shared this with me?"

"Because you would've teased me about it, and I never would've heard the end of it. I think your job is pretty cool. You're actually making a difference in the community and working with the youth. Our business isn't really kid friendly."

Calvin chuckled. "This is true. Well of course I'll help interview. I created a question guide so we can use that. Am I going to have to trademark the materials I send you so you don't steal it under the 'family title'?"

Coraline stuffed her mouth quickly and shook her head no.

"Okay then. Well, I hope you spoke with someone in HR."

"We use a third party for HR, HHH. Humans helping helpers, something like that. I know our account specialist is Leila. She called me last week and I've been meaning to call her back. My brain has just been all over the place. I'll call her this week to set up a meeting to review a job description for the posting."

"Yea, also go over the budget for the position and get it posted asap. I'm sure we can find a secretary or office manager in the next two months. It's the summer time so we could maybe even start a paid internship for the Fall semester. Leila should have a college recruiter contact."

Coraline pushed his chest out of excitement. "That's a great idea! Maybe even for HBCU students too!"

"Ouch," he said annoyed, rubbing his chest. He preferred the bruises Gemini gave him.

"We would have someone to mentor and build. College grads are eager, and we aren't a 'traditional' company anyway." She blew out air. "You're right. Thank you for your help, the whole HR piece was really messing with me. I forgot we paid a company to handle that. It's hard managing the budget, release schedules, maintaining the inventory for the online store. I don't want to expand to anymore locations for at least eight more months. I need to get a good office manager in here and train them and myself at the same time." She placed her plate in the sink. "Also, about Gemini, think of something she would enjoy and get rid of the old fucking bonnet."

Calvin rubbed his forehead. "I already did that."

"Good. You've already introduced her to us and if you messed this up, I'm beating your ass. So please think with your head. Mom liked her a lot." He nodded. He knew Gemini well enough to give her a good gift. That meant he was going to have to make a few stops to prepare. He hasn't heard from her in over a week and each day made the anxiety in his stomach grow.

Chapter Twenty-One

Gemini

Gemini sat on her apartment balcony, looking at the trees around the complex. She was thankful it was finally Saturday. The sounds of outdoors helped her relax. Feeling the sun on her skin rather than the florescent lights was what she needed.

It's been two weeks since she'd seen or spoken to Calvin. Her phone has been quiet and she missed his efforts. She still couldn't bring herself to block his number, but she had a good reason to be pissed off. What if that girl, had lice or dirty hair. She knew Calvin probably never washed it. Why did he even still have it? She had even more questions that needed answers.

But then again, the static between them was hard to ignore. She genuinely missed his arms around her, the random kisses on her neck while she pretended to be asleep. She was tired of running. It was time to open her mouth and ears. Too much time had passed.

Gemini: Can we talk?

Calvin: Of course! Can I come over?

Gemini: Sure.

Calvin was pulling into her complex not even 15 minutes later. She just finished rolling a blunt when she saw his car pull up. She got up and opened the door before he could knock. He stared her in the eye. There he goes with that breathless look in his face. His beard was starting to come as a shadow and he looked tired. Was he going through hell too? *Good.*

She had to stop herself from leaping in his arms and dragging him to her bedroom. She took a deep breath, "Are you okay with sitting on the balcony? I was about to smoke."

He nodded. "Yea that's fine."

She opened the door wider for him. When he walked in his eyes were wide. "Wow your place looks even better in person." Constance meowed loudly at him. He bent down and scratched the top of her head. Constance leaned into his hand, lightly nudging her head. *Traitor.* It's hard to be mad at him when he played with her cat. She was about to give him a look, but this was his first time inside. Gemini wasn't always keen on letting people invade her space. She preferred going to his house. She took another deep breath as she slid open the door to the balcony. Constance decided that her tree would be more fun.

Watching Calvin sit in the other patio seat was surreal. Why did he have to wear a black t-shirt? It's hugging his shoulders in all the right places. His eyes hidden behind his black framed glasses. If she saw his back, she would fold. There is something about black men in black. *Remember you're pissed off!*

"So, you're ready to talk?" he asked looking at her.

She cleared her throat. "Yes, I am. I have a few questions and I want direct answers. Can you do that?" He nodded, rubbing his hands on his knees as he leaned back. His nails scratching his leg like how he scratched her ass and back. *Focus.* "How long were you single before we met?"

"Technically 6 weeks and 4 days, if you want me to be specific."

She nodded her head. "And y'all were together for 3 years?

"Yea."

"And she worked with your family business, that I now know is not in finance. Does she still work there?"

"No, she quit two days after we broke up. Gemini, I can't apologize enough. I didn't mean to offend you by giving you her bonnet. I got rid of all of her stuff besides her bonnet because I honestly forgot about it."

She squinted her eyes at him. "Did you wash it?"

"I did, it smelled like her moisturizer and I hated it. So I washed everything when she moved out. The sheets, the carpet, hell I even washed the walls."

"Why did y'all break up?" She lit the blunt and brought it to her lips.

Calvin sighed. "We met before I started my master's program. She was getting her MBA and needed an internship so I introduced her to Coraline. They became close friends and

Coraline talked mom into creating a job for her and everything. Shortly after we moved in together, I thought everything was cool. I wasn't ring shopping but I was saving up for it. Since we were in school at the same time, I was busy, she was busy, and we would sometimes study in separate places. I'd be in the living room, she in the office or vice versa.

"One night, she said she was headed to a coffee shop to study. I said okay. Then, when an hour passed, I decided to pick up some flowers to surprise her and study with her. But when I pulled up, I didn't see her car and she wasn't inside. We never shared our location, but I had my ways. I drove and went to her location, and it was a house a few minutes away from her campus. Her car was in the driveway. I didn't want to assume anything so I just sat across the street, staring at the house. Then, a light turned on upstairs and a couple stepped outside on the balcony. I could tell it was obviously her and a man." His knuckles tightened, she passed him the blunt. As he hit it, the bones in his face tightened. Gemini could tell he needed this. "He bent her over the side and fucked her from the back. I could- I could hear and see it. I know what she sounds like. He even said her fucking name so she couldn't deny it." *Damn.*

She put her hand on top of his. "I'm so sorry Calvin. That sucks to find out your partner cheated. Did you recognize the house?"

"No. I didn't even tell her I went. I took a picture of her car in his driveway, threw the flowers out of the window and left. We dated for three more months before I even broke up with her. I was emotionally checked out and she didn't even notice. We hadn't had sex the last six months of our relationship anyway. So, when it was official, it didn't really faze me. I didn't cheat or anything, I just got used her being around." He passed the blunt back to Gemini.

She understood not wanting to talk about the past in a new relationship. Hell, she hasn't gone into specifics either, she couldn't judge him too harshly. Her feelings were already so attached to him. "I forgive you. I honestly missed you a lot. I've gotten used to talking to you."

His eyes twinkled. "Really? I missed you too more than you really know. Whew okay now I have to give you something, I'll be right back." He ran out of the door and down the steps to his car. He pulled out a bouquet. *Of course, the average flower trick.*

She put the blunt out on the ashtray as she heard her front door open and close.

"Gem, you are unique and beautiful. So I had to make you something as special as you." He turned the bouquet and there were books embedded with the fresh flowers. There are at least six books and it was the most beautiful thing she had scene.

She gasped as she brushed her fingers on the covers. Her jaw dropped as she opened the first pages, they were all signed editions. "These weren't flowers that could be left on your doorstep."

"All of these novels are signed!? Jasmine Guillory, Talia Hibbert and A.E. Valdez? How did you do this?"

"I wanted to gift you with a curated book collection with your favorite authors. I didn't know what books you had already, so I had to make it special."

She got up, holding the arrangement and sat on his lap. His arm wrapped around her as they should. "Okay all is forgiven. I can't be mad in front of the books. Its disrespectful."

Calvin put his hand on her chin, brushing his thumb across her jaw. "Were good? I'm your man again?"

"You were always my man baby. But you don't have a secret child or anything right?"

He chuckled, "Not that I know of. I promise to be more forthcoming with information, even if it's too much. I can't go that long without you in my life again."

Gemini half smiled at him. A rare breeze blew against their skin as she looked him in his eye. Maybe he was worth it. He was worth the chance at love.

He brought his thumb to her face and brushed her right cheek. Her skin felt like it was tingling, removing her from her thoughts. Then he leaned into her and kissed her lightly on the lips, like she was too tempting of a sweet treat. She placed the book bouquet on her chair and wrapped her arms around his neck, kissing him deeper. He planted his hands firmly on her ass and squeezed as he moaned in her mouth. She grazed her teeth across his bottom lip and sucked it.

Calvin pressed his hands firmly on her hips and waist. He slowly pulled away from the kiss to whisper in her ear, "Can I keep showing you how much I missed you?"

Heat filled her entire body to her toes, "Oh you missed me?"

"You know I did Gemini," he said against the skin on her neck. "I've learned my lesson. I'll write a book about my life story so you can know everything that has happened to me. I'm all yours."

Another smile danced on her lips, "I'd be glad to read it and ask follow up questions. I'm all yours too."

They walked back inside her apartment as Gemini guided Calvin to her bedroom.

Epilogue
A Year Later

Gemini and Calvin covered the master bedroom floor with plastic, preparing to paint the walls an earthy green color. Since Gemini officially moved in 6 months ago, when her lease ended, she had different suggestions for their house. After doing hours of YouTube research, she wanted to make her mark. Their degrees were already on proud display in their office. The projects they have done so far include mulching part of the backyard, installing new peel and stick tile to the master bathroom and now updating the bedrooms. Gemini already ordered a TV Wall mount for their room.

They were wearing matching paint-stained overalls as they carefully poured the paint and began rolling it on the walls. "I have a random question Calvin."

He looked towards her, "What's up?"

"What made you attracted to a girl like me? I mean I was literally reading at the bar when we met."

He put the paint brush roller back in the pan and walked towards her. She put her roller in the pan too. He squeezed her hands. "I happen to like my woman and all her quirks. How you read in public places, to your sweet and savory snacks that have taken over the pantry." She laughed. "And you are clearly beautiful. I had to make my move, even though that wasn't my intention going to the bar that day."

"So you don't regret meeting me?" Gemini asked rocking on her heels.

"Hell no, you've brought too much good in my life to be a regret Gem. I love you."

She smiled, "I love you too."

A few weeks later, Calvin hosted a barbeque and invited everyone important. From his mom and sisters, Greg and even Aunt Lorraine. Gemini walked around greeting everyone in a beautiful yellow sundress. Serena even came into town which made Gemini even more excited. In the year they spent together, they grew in more ways than one. She was being more vulnerable and open, while Calvin was her constant listening ear. Then came time for an announcement.

"Good evening everyone!" Calvin yelled holding his cup in the air. "Thank you for coming to our cookout. We are so glad you came to spend some time with us. I just want to take some time to say thank you to my wonderful, beautiful girlfriend Gemini. She's the reason why the house looks so nice!" Everyone

laughed and she awkwardly waved next to him. He put his arm around her waist. "I appreciate her for turning my house, into our home. I am truly thankful I met someone as amazing, creative and smart as her."

He placed his cup down on the counter, reached his hand in his pocket and pulled out a ring box as he got down on one knee. Gemini squealed as he grabbed her left hand, brushing her knuckles with his thumb. "Will you do me the honor of marrying me Gemini Collins? You are the love of my life."

Her eyes began to fill with tears. If she thought reading at a bar brought her this kind of man, she would do it all over again. Shout out to Greg for convincing him to go out that night. Greg and his fiancé were standing behind the crowd. She looked up at Aunt Lorraine who was smiling with tears in her eyes. Serena was next to her Aunt jumping up and down, clapping. Gemini screamed yes and the group cheered. The Grants were on the other side. Ms. Grant's hand was on her heart, Casey was recording and Coraline held a thumbs up and smiled.

Calvin placed the diamond cut ring on her left ring finger. She bent down and kissed him, crashing her lips against his in excitement. Then they hugged and fell on the floor. Everyone joined in helping them back up.

After everyone left, Gemini sat on Calvin's lap on their couch, reading another smutty novel. Calvin had a horror novel in his grasp. The lamp on above them, a blanket in her lap. His glasses brushing the side of her face. She was happy to share her life with someone. Constance leapt onto the couch, Calvin petted her smiling down. Now, time to plan a wedding. It was the start of something new.

Acknowledgments

I finished my first novel! (Megan thee Stallion ahh). First and foremost I want to thank God for everything. I have always dreamed of sharing my words so I also thank God for the ability to write and the confidence to share my words and ideas. As a child, I always dreamed of becoming an author and it's finally coming true.

I also want to thank my husband for his love, support and encouragement to be myself in my writing. Also, for being patient when ideas are running around my head at 100 mph. While I was in the final process of editing this novelette, I became pregnant and gave birth to our beautiful daughter. Thank you Antonio for always reminding me who I am as a person and as a mother.

I also want to thank my mother, grandmother and grandfather for gifting me my first laptop. It allowed me to write and express myself in ways that created a path for me to be here. It changed my outlook and allowed me to fall in love with writing in a new way.

Thank you to Shae with Stala Designs on the beautiful book cover, Alli with Falcon Faerie Fiction for beta reading and editing and Lauren with Sunflower Rose Publishing for formatting.

Finally, I would also like to thank all of my sisters, friends, online and in person, for the constant love and inspiration. This is the first of many works!

About the Author

A Florida born, Georgia living author with home library dreams.

Kirahvi holds a BA in Psychology and MBA in Healthcare Administration. After finishing her degrees, she fell back in love with reading and writing romance novels. Her favorite places are a cozy secluded cabin or playing in the water at the beach. They spent most of their childhood reading and writing short stories.

Kirahvi spends their free time in the library, reading at the park, walking through a museum, creating book content or listening to vinyl's with their husband and daughter. The family waves their Tampa Bay Buccaneers flag high. You can find her on all social media outlets

@Kirahvi_Reads or her website www.kirahvibello.com for more information.